MADDY YIP'S

GUIDE TO HOLIDAYS

STORY and PICTURES by Sue Cheung

ANDERSEN PRESS

First published in 2022 by
Andersen Press Limited
20 Vauxhall Bridge Road, London SW1V 2SA, UK
Vijverlaan 48, 3062 HL, Rotterdam, Nederland
www.andersenpress.co.uk

2 4 6 8 10 9 7 5 3 1

British Library Cataloguing in Publication Data available.

ISBN 978 1 83913 197 4

Printed and bound in Great Britain by Clays Ltd,
Elcograf S.p.A.

MADDY YIP'S

GUIDE TO HOLIDAYS

To Rhian,
who I imagine to be Maddy
in a parallel universe, and if
that's the case, then I am Dev.

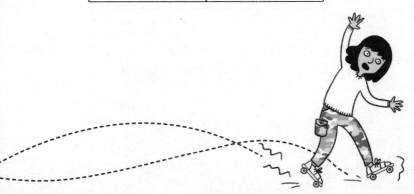

DEV

(BEZZIE FRIEND)

Shall I compare thee to a marshmallow?

FUZZFACE

A stray cat that won't go away

GED SPONGER

while crushing a brick into dust

Eating MY chocolate

HULK

Oli's scabby guinea pig

Sunday

School **Easter** holidays had only just begun and I already wanted to stick my head in a bucket of frogspawn.

Correction, a *wok* full of **frogspawn**. Because unlike other families who might have a proper frog pond, we have one made out of a Chinese frying pan. Dad doesn't like chucking anything out, so he had a **brainwave** to reuse the wok after I ruined it burning an omelette.

He says he likes saving nature, but we all know it's really the pennies he's trying to save!

The **Easter** holidays were boring but I didn't complain out loud because if I do Mam always thinks of chores for me, normally involving bins, and I wasn't doing that *rubbish*! **(HA! HA!)**

I went upstairs to hide and my little brother Oli was in our bedroom (because we share, worst luck).

'What are you doing?' I said.

'Counting my **Easter** eggs,' he replied.

He only had four, I could see that as soon as I walked in. **BLIMEY**, he must have been more bored than I was! He was prodding the eggs with his **Luke Skywalker** action figure's hand as he counted. Then he recounted just to make sure.

UGH.

I don't care which comes first but *pleeaase*:

1) Can I have my own bedroom?

2) Can the holidays be over so I don't have to put up with this madness?!

I headed back downstairs but my big brother Jack heard me **shriek** outside his room as I trod in a lump of homemade slime Oli had dropped on the carpet.

'Oi, Nut, come here!' he shouted.

I wish he would stop calling me that. That 'peanut up my nose' incident was over six years ago. I am not that person any more. I am now intelligent, mature and fully aware of the correct hole food goes into. I opened his door and huffed, **'WHAT?'**

'You got any snacks?' he said, staring at his computer screen.

Anyone who blatantly insults me then asks for snacks without saying 'please' can go for a naked jog in a cactus field as far as I am concerned.

'Ah no, sorry I haven't,' I lied.

Dev, my bezzie mate who goes to drama club, taught me how to look sorry by thinking of something tragic. So while lying to Jack I thought about that family picnic where I accidentally trod on the hem of my skirt as I stood up and ended up **faceplanting** in the soft cheese swirl. Nobody came to my rescue as I lay suffocating in a stinking lump of **curdled gloop** because they were laughing so much. **CRETINS.**

YAAAH!

'Ask Oli if I can have one of his eggs,' said Jack, making a banana **KUNG FU KICK** a guava on his computer game.

I said, **'ASK HIM YOURSELF, WASSOCK!'** and scarpered downstairs before he could catch me. It was the most fun I'd had all morning.

Grandad was in his converted garage room doing a thousand-piece baked bean jigsaw without his specs on. He is as **blind as a bat**, so I had no idea how he'd already completed half the puzzle. We call him Agung which is 'Grandad' in Chinese, well Hakka, to be specific, as Dad says there's different dialects. He's the only one in our family who can talk to

Agung properly because he speaks Hakka too. I helped Agung with the jigsaw for thirty seconds before realising that sitting in a bath full of actual baked beans would be less torturous.

Ahhhhh...

I had run out of rooms to mope about in, so I ventured out to the back garden. Our mangy old cat **FUZZFACE** was having a wee on Agung's freshly dug veg patch ready for planting his pak choi. I think I will pass on the pak choi when it ends up on my plate.

I peered through the shed window. Dad was at work but I wanted to check how his latest hobby project was going. He is building a bicycle-powered potato chipper and intends to make millions. Yeah, *millions* of customers angry about the **mess** it makes!

He will never leave his job as a warehouse manager at the car metal parts factory though. I once asked him why he stays in a job he doesn't particularly like and he replied, 'It gets me out of this madhouse, doesn't it?!' Then it occurred to me – so **THAT'S** why parents go to work.

Something brushed against my foot and when I looked down, **FUZZFACE** had deposited half a chewed worm on my shoe. I was thinking how much worse **Easter** holidays could get when Dev appeared in his back garden, one over from ours. Well, at first I thought Mr Sharma had planted a gigantic rose bush, until I realised it was Dev swathed in a floral shawl.

'Hey Maddy, what's up?' he said.

'THIS!' I said, holding my shoe aloft and pointing to the offending slime. 'And this!' I picked up **FUZZFACE** and pointed at her face, which turned out to be her backside. (She is so shaggy it is hard to tell which end is which sometimes.)

Dev invited me over to his and when I got there, it turned out he was going *insane* with boredom too.

'There must be loads of stuff we can do,' he said.

'Let's do a brainstorm,' I said. 'What do you think of when I say the word **Easter**?'

'Fluffy chicks?' he said.

'We could visit the petting farm?'

'I can't, feathers set off my asthma,' said Dev.

Well that put an end to that. I thought about Oli's **Easter** eggs and had an idea.

'Hey, remember that great granny who broke the Guinness World Record by cramming all those marshmallows into her gob?' I said.

'Yeah?'

'Well, why don't we invent The Plunkthorpe World Records and eat as many **Easter** eggs as we can in one go?'

'**Eggs-cellent** idea! Any **eggs-cuse** to scoff stupid amounts of chocolate,' said Dev.

'At last, the **Easter** holidays are getting **eggs-citing**,' I answered, overdoing the **egg joke** ever so slightly. The only problem was we didn't have any eggs, so we scraped together some pocket money to buy some.

We caught the bus into town and went straight to the **NINETY-NINE PENCE SHOP.** There was a choice between small *luxury* eggs or the more inferior gigantic ones. We plumped for five giant ones as we weren't fussy about eating products made from the sweepings-up off the factory floor, plus this was all about quantity not quality. While waiting in the queue to pay, Dev did one of his overly dramatic gasps and pointed to the wall behind me. **'NO . . . WAY!'** he cried out. I turned to see a poster advertising a new ride at Sudmouth Amusement Park with the words:

WILL YOU **SURVIVE** AN **ENCOUNTER** WITH THE **MEGA BEAST ?!**

'We have to go!' Dev squeaked, jiggling up and down.

I sighed. 'Don't be daft, our parents won't shell out for a trip to Sudmouth. They won't even pay for quilted bog roll.'

We paid for the eggs but the prospect of guzzling them didn't seem so appealing after seeing that poster which showed us what

REAL excitement was all about. To add to the misery we bumped into Ted and Tod, the horrid toddler twins, outside the shop with their mam. I said 'Hello', but all I could think

of was shielding the contents of my bag. If **EVIL TWINS** found out I had a tonne of chocolate eggs in there, they would crowbar my bedroom door off to get at them. Mam, who is their childminder, says they won't go in my room, but I found their jammy fingerprints all over my old *Etch A Sketch* just last Friday.

Ted had a sly snoop in my bag and shouted, 'Choc-let!'

Then Tod screeched, 'Gimme!'

BRILLIANT.

I said, 'Sorry, can't stop', then edged away while dragging Dev behind me.

As we were waiting at the bus stop another nightmare appeared around the corner.

'Oh no, it's Ged Sponger and he's flipping seen us!' Dev whispered loudly.

Ged is always trying to take stuff off us.

'Hey, Yip, what's in your bag?' Ged grunted as he approached.

I thought quickly and babbled, 'Horse excrement for my grandad's pak choi.'

It worked because Ged looked baffled then disgusted, then stomped off in a huff. **HA!** It's so easy to outsmart the **biggest plonker** in **Plunkthorpe**.

During the bus journey home me and Dev discussed how many ways we could find to go on **THE MEGA BEAST**, but the pathetic conclusion we came to was **NONE**. The next most important topic was how to keep the eggs away from the thieving twins.

'Can you store them at yours?' I said to Dev.

'Er hello . . . **Canine Hoover**?' he replied.

Dev was referring to his dog Graham, who gets taken to the vet at least once a year with 'intestinal obstruction' i.e. he mistakes things like **dental floss** and **elastic bands** for tasty treats, which then bung up his insides. Last time it was an entire pack of Dev's little sister Heena's plasticine and he

WHOO-WHOO-WHOOOOOOOOOO!!!

did **Technicolored poop** for a week. Heena said only unicorns poop rainbows, so Graham must be a 'magical wonder'. Not at three hundred pounds per vet's bill he's not!

I took the eggs back to my house in the end and hoped by some miracle that **EVIL TWINS** didn't get their grubby little mitts on them.

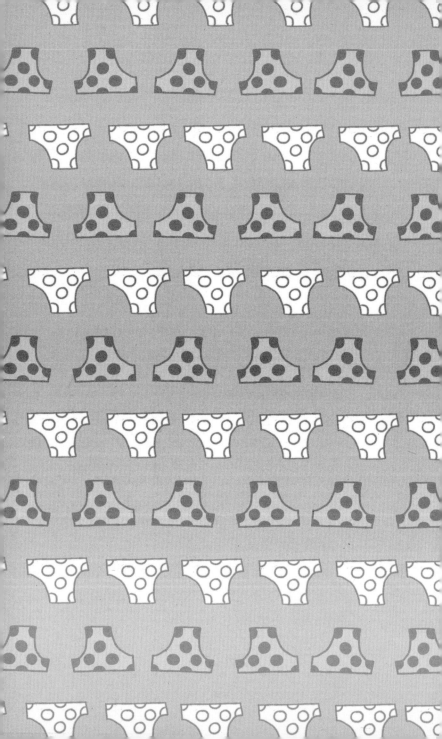

Monday – way too early

Mam burst into my room at seven o'clock this morning. **I was appalled!** Doesn't she know that growing kids need **twenty-three hours of sleep** a night in order to develop into well-adjusted adults? (Unlike her!) I read that in a magazine last 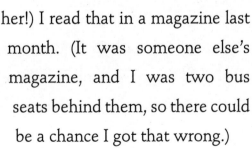 month. (It was someone else's magazine, and I was two bus seats behind them, so there could be a chance I got that wrong.)

Mam said she was cleaning. The woman is **POSSESSED**! Actually the real reason for Mam's erratic behaviour was because the childminding inspectors were coming and the house needed to be immaculate. I reminded her they weren't due till after the **Easter** holidays, which was ages away. She ignored me, drew the curtains back and snapped, **'What are your pants doing on the windowsill?!'**

'They need airing,' I mumbled, from under the pillow that I had placed over my head to drown out the noise of dusting.

Really, I'd had to find somewhere to put the **Easter** eggs me and Dev bought yesterday. So I'd emptied a clothes drawer and put them in there.

'The neighbours don't want to see your **disgusting undies**,' said Mam. 'They'll think we're a **bunch of scruffs**!'

Well if they were 'disgusting' then I blamed it on the knackered old washer (not Mam, the washing machine). I got up to clear them away and spotted the rusty cement mixer and bashed-up scooter that Dad couldn't fit into his shed sprawled over the lawn. I pointed them out to Mam. 'Now that's what I call a **pile of pants!**'

'Don't worry, I've already had words with Dad about *that* eyesore!' said Mam.

Oli woke up and started whinging about the noise, which ironically just added to the existing noise. (I have decided that when I get my own room I will have a huge party and invite everyone . . . except Oli). I opened my drawer and stared blankly into it. I was having a dilemma about how to fit my drawers into my drawers! **HA! HA!** Then the doorbell rang.

'Who's got the nerve to go bothering people at this ungodly hour?' said my mother, who came into *my* room at *seven* in the morning to polish the radiator pipes with a cotton bud! **'Go and see who that idiot is and tell them to do one!'** she said.

I went downstairs and answered the door. It was Mrs Tatlock dropping the **EVIL TWINS** off early for childminding.

'Oh, hello, Mrs Tatlock, I forgot you were coming early today!' Mam puffed, racing down the stairs.

She was doing one of her weird toothy smiles. The Tatlocks are the best employers Mam's ever had, so she becomes uncharacteristically nice whenever they are round. The twins are also oddly well-behaved, right up until the very second their parents leave, then they turn our house into the **Chester Zoo chimp enclosure**.

As soon as Mrs Tatlock had left and Mam had disappeared into the kitchen to make breakfast, **EVIL TWINS** were straight onto me.

'Gim-me choc-let!' snarled Ted.

It is quite unnerving to be cornered by a three-and-a-half year old. Dev said the twins are like Chihuahuas. Their bark is normally worse than their bite. But what Dev doesn't know is that I have had a terrifying **Chihuahua phobia** ever since Jack told me that they have the ability to leap on you from their lairs (normally bins) and gouge your eyes out with their secret chin tusks.

I put my bravest face on and replied, 'What Chihuahua . . . I mean . . . chocolate?'

'Easter eeeggs!' squealed Tod.

'Oh **THOSE!**' I said. 'Sorry, I've given them away to the naked mole rat charity. Mole rats can only eat chocolate like pandas can only eat bamboo, you know.'

For a moment I thought I'd succeeded in flummoxing them, because they shut up for a few joyous seconds.

Then Oli blabbed, 'But I saw your **Easter** eggs in your undies drawer just a minute ago!'

AMAZING.

Maybe my **Easter** egg money would have been put to better use if I'd paid to get Oli's mouth clamped. And as if the morning hadn't got off to a bad enough start, Mam shouted from the kitchen, 'Maddy, Agung wants to go to the garden centre today so I thought you could take him on the bus. I've left money on the hallway table.'

FANTASTIC.

I was about to moan about it when she added, 'Oh, and take Oli too!'

UGH.

I was thinking I'd rather be out of the house than have to put up with **EVIL TWINS** so I answered, 'Well all right, but make sure the twins don't go in my room!'

'They won't, I've warned them,' said Mam.

That means nothing. A couple of weeks ago, I finally managed to persuade Dad to put a bolt on my door after they'd blatantly rummaged through my bedside drawer. I know because every single page of my *Little Book of Staying Absolutely Calm in Any Situation* was smeared with Ted's unmistakable luminous green snot.

Dad thinks I exaggerate about their **evilness**. He said, 'They're only wee pipsqueaks, what harm can they do?'

They had already done the following in the space of **an hour** this morning:

1) Squished their breakfast out of the letterbox, which caused all our post to arrive covered in raspberry fromage frais.

2) Inserted a sock into the DVD player tray which has activated a permanent DISC ERROR message.

3) Stuck a sheet of *Fun time with pets!* stickers all over **FUZZFACE**, which we are still in the process of unpeeling.

Play a little game...

Simple Simon says 'sit still for ever into infinity'

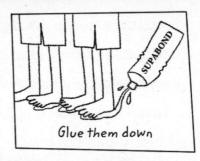

Glue them down

SUPABOND

Lock yourself in the shed

SMASH!

Send them on a nice holiday

TO PLUTO (NO RETURN POSTAGE)

- Help!

Dad's normally at work when **EVIL TWINS** are around so he misses most of the carnage. Even though I made sure he put the door bolt high up where they couldn't reach, it was a **massive FAIL**. The other day Jack went home from school at dinnertime to fetch a textbook and caught them undoing it. Ted was standing on a footstool on top of a toy crate on top of a chair, and was prodding the bolt loose with a cucumber. They are **SHOCKINGLY** enterprising master criminals (the twins, not cucumbers). When Jack asked what they were doing, Ted flung the cucumber at him and screamed, 'BIG BOY NASTY!'

Mam went to see what all the commotion was about and it was Jack that got into trouble, for wasting good vegetables! Apparently Mam hadn't even realised the twins were gone. One minute she was washing up and they were colouring at the kitchen table, the next minute they'd disappeared. Well, if they were going to play games, then I had no other choice than to use the same tactic back. But first I needed to call Dev and tell him the situation.

'I've got to take Agung and Oli out and the twins know the eggs are in my room. What shall I do?' I said.

Dev paused for a moment then replied, 'Remember that film we watched where they used booby traps to catch intruders?'

'Yeah?' I said, recalling it vaguely.

'One of the traps was a bucket of water balanced over a slightly open door,' he continued. 'And when the intruders tried to enter, the bucket tipped over and totally soaked them!'

'**GENIUS!**' I cried. 'What else could I do?'

'Don't you think that's enough?' said Dev.

'NO! Come on, this is **EVIL TWINS** we're talking about!' I said, getting into the swing of it.

'OK, another trick is to put a load of flour behind the door so when the intruders break in, they leave a trail of footsteps and that way you know they've been.'

'*Eggs*-cellent!' I replied.

I couldn't wait to set the traps. **EVIL TWINS** needed to be taught a lesson for once.

'Hey,' said Dev, changing the subject. 'Have you thought any more about **THE MEGA BEAST**?'

'What, about how we're **NEVER** going to go on it? *No*, don't be a divvy, Dev.'

'Yeah, I suppose you're right,' sighed Dev. 'We might as well forget about it.'

I thanked Dev for his cunning input, hung up and went straight to the kitchen to get a bucket of water and bag of flour. If **EVIL TWINS** fall into my traps, the thrill of it would more than make up for not going on **THE MEGA BEAST**!

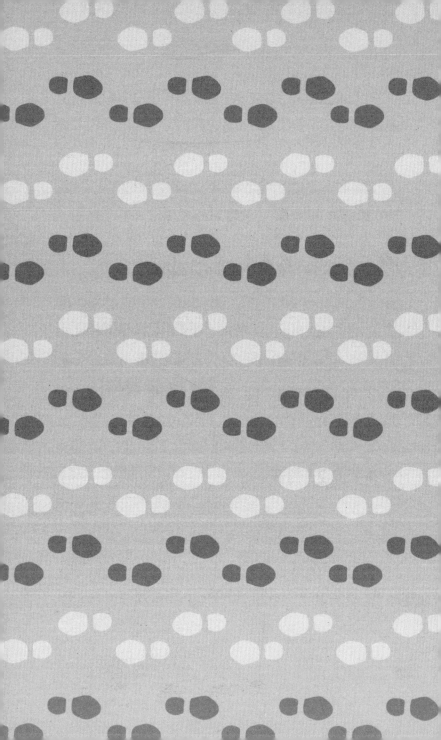

Monday – later that day

It took ages to get to the garden centre because of Agung's sciatica. He needed to sit down fourteen times for a rest, and that was only to the bus stop.

AMAZING.

The garden centre was dead busy when we got there. Mostly full of pensioners looking for a free day out. I don't understand what the appeal

is myself. There is nothing remotely interesting about **woody perennials** or **Victorian trellises**, and to top it all off the place smells like a pile of rotten manure.

I found the ornaments section quite entertaining though, due to the puzzling array of useless tat on display. Right now you can get resin hedgehogs wearing cloth caps at half price, and if you buy a camper van-shaped watering can you get a free glow-in-the-dark toadstool with it. **HIDEOUS!** No wonder they were trying to give them away!

I spotted a badly painted gnome with a monobrow and pointed it out to Agung.

'Look, it's Jack!' I said.

He laughed so hard his teeth fell out into a terrarium full of cacti and I had to fetch a member of staff to help us retrieve them. She ended up putting on weeding gloves and using a trowel to pluck them out. She didn't seem very pleased about the whole ordeal. I wanted to point out that it said *'Happy to help with anything!'* on her badge, but thought best not to push it.

After we wiped the soil off Agung's teeth and he put them back in, we traipsed about for another half an hour until he **finally** bought something, which turned out to be one piddly packet of tomato seeds! I couldn't believe I'd given up half my day for this when I should have been guarding my Easter eggs and preparing to break a local record. As we made our way towards the exit I wondered what the status was with my *booby traps*. The twins could have had a very nasty surprise by now. Then I had a dreadful thought, I forgot to tell Jack what I was up to. What if he walked into the traps instead? I came to the conclusion that it would:

a) Serve him right for being a sneaky thief
b) Mean my life wasn't going to be worth living when I got back!

Agung tugged my sleeve and said something in Chinese. He pointed to the café and rubbed his belly. That meant he wanted to stop for lunch.

GREAT.

Anyone who's ever had a meal with Agung knows he eats at the speed of a tortoise and **weirdly**, chews like one too. I always half expect him to suddenly retract his head at the slightest hint of danger. It is quite disturbing.

'I'm hungry too,' said Oli. 'And so is Luke.'

'How can Luke be hungry when he's a doll?' I said.

'He's not a *doll*, he's an
ACTION FIGURE!' said
Oli, thrusting the swivel-eyed
Jedi at me.

'OK, no need to get *hangry*!'
I said.

'Wha . . . ?'

'Anger made worse by hunger, Oli.'

'Wha . . . ?'

UGH.

Never mind breaking the record for scoffing
Easter eggs. I was already breaking the record

for having the dimwittest brother **EVER**. I knew Oli would probably tell Mam if I didn't feed his big **blabbermouth**, so I took him and Agung to the café.

As I choked my dry-as-sawdust sausage roll down with my weak lukewarm tea, I thought about all those lucky people who would get to go on the wicked **MEGA BEAST** ride this fortnight. I felt a lake of tears well up in my eye . . . until I realised I'd **ACCIDENTALLY** rubbed brown sauce into it.

We'd been gone almost four hours by the time we got back home. Agung could have planted those tomato seeds at the start of our trip and had a fully fruiting veg patch by now!

Mam was in the kitchen with **EVIL TWINS** so I tiptoed upstairs to check on the trap situation. Sure enough the snooping gits had been in my room, but I had forgotten one crucial detail: flour and water mixed together makes glue! And if left to dry for long enough, it turns into solid cement! The bucket of water had tipped

straight onto the heap of flour, then from what I could gather, the twins had done a full-on **JIG** on top of it because footprints were stomped all over my room and the landing, and the dark blue carpet only made the white splodges look a **gazillion** times worse.

The twins had taken their mucky boots off at the top of the stairs before they went back down, and that's why Mam hadn't suspected anything yet.

I tried to scrape some of the cement off with my shoe, but it was stiffer than the quinoa crust pizza Mam made last night. Then I remembered about the chocolate eggs and went to check in the drawer. Two of them had been **smashed** and eaten – **DEVIL CHILDREN**!

I was worrying about what Dev would say when Oli sauntered in. **'MAM'S GONNA KILL YOU,'** he said.

'DON'T TELL AND I'LL GIVE YOU THESE!' I said, piling the rest of the eggs into his arms.

'OK, ta!' he chirped, and skipped off to his side of the room behind the divider curtain.

Forget about Mam killing me, I was going to get crucified by Dev for **failing** to safeguard our eggs. A minute later I heard the twins totter into the hallway downstairs and Mam saying, 'Let's go upstairs and find your boots.'

NOOOO!

I tried to come up with an excuse but my brain was **BLANK WITH PANIC**. Footsteps reached the top of the stairs, then I braced myself . . .

'WHAT THE HELL IS THIS?!!' Mam shrieked.

IT WAS THE TWINS!' I blurted. 'If they hadn't been snooping about, this wouldn't have happened.'

'But . . . the *childminding inspectors*!' said Mam, clamping her head in her hands.

'I'll get it cleaned up, honest!' I whimpered.

I wasn't sure how, as I wasn't in possession of an industrial pickaxe.

The only way I could make up for the damage was by giving up my pocket money for (quick calculation) . . . **EVER!**

After the twins were collected by Mr Tatlock, I explained what had happened to Mam and she **ranted**: 'What's your dad going to say when he sees this? He's back in half an hour and the carpet's **WRECKED** with . . . with . . . what even *is* this stuff?!'

'Flour and water,' I mumbled.

'Oh god,' she groaned. 'Well, I suppose it's my fault too. I promised the twins wouldn't go in your room.'

Moments later Dad came home from work. When he plodded upstairs and saw us both scrubbing away, he said, **'What's all this mess?'**

'My fault,' I said.

'Mine too,' Mam said.

'OK, no need to cover up for the **devious duo**,' said Dad. 'I know it was them because somehow my potato chipper invention is covered in fromage frais.'

At last, Dad is aware of their **EVILNESS**!

'Great timing though,' he added.

Me and Mam glanced at each other, puzzled, and Mam replied, 'What do you mean?'

Dad said, 'A mate at work told me today where I can get a cracking deal on new carpet. Right *luxury stuff* too. We could pull up this manky one and replace it.'

'Brand new carpet . . . for *cheap*?' said Mam, suddenly perking up. She was up for anything to make the house look better, especially if she didn't have to fork out full price for it.

'Aye,' said Dad. 'We could easily lay it between the two of us. Thing is, the kids'll have to be out of the house for a few days while it's being done.'

'Well, I'm sure that can be sorted,' said Mam, clapping her hands together gleefully.

PHEW, talk about a lucky escape!

Tuesday

Dad took time off work this morning, drove to the carpet store where they were having a closing down sale and bought a brand-new roll of thick, cream-coloured carpet for half price. It was sitting in the hallway when I got home after fetching Oli from football practice. When no one was looking I went over and ran my fingers through its luxurious fibres. I imagine it was like stroking a sheep, but without the stench of silage or being plagued by ticks.

The thought of soft new carpet underfoot filled me with joy, (mainly because our existing one had a lump of chewing gum stuck to it right where I get out of bed every morning), but it wasn't life changing, like **THE MEGA BEAST** would be. I mean, what could even come close to going on a ride with three corkscrews, five bumps and a twenty-metre drop?

Before dinner the family gathered around the kitchen table to discuss the incredibly dull topic

of floor refurbishments. Our parents are very keen on home improvements these days. But it's not because of their love of interior decor, it's because **EVIL TWINS** leave the house in a constant state of ruin. Admittedly the carpet was one quarter my fault (the second quarter being the twins', the third Mam's for trusting the twins, and the fourth Dev's for suggesting the well dodgy idea in the first place).

'Right,' said Mam. 'As me and your dad have got several days off work, we've decided to get the carpet laid this **Easter** weekend.'

'But where can we get rid of you lot?' said Dad.

'Easy for me. I can go to Dev's,' I said.

'I'm staying at Gav's,' said Jack.

Jack won't admit it but he wanted to stay at Gav's just because he happened to live next door to Kayla Digby, who Jack thinks he's going out with when really she insists they are just book club pals – **WHAT A CHUMP!**

'What about me?' said Oli.

Agung slurped his oolong tea and **BURPED**. It was all right for him, he didn't need to go anywhere. He had his perfect self-contained room, complete with high definition TV and double toasted sandwich maker, to lounge around in.

'Well, I was thinking you could all stay at Aunt Pat's,' said Mam.

BRILLIANT.

Pat is a far distant relative of Mam's who dedicates her life to collecting Tupperware. At last count, she had 2,478 containers.

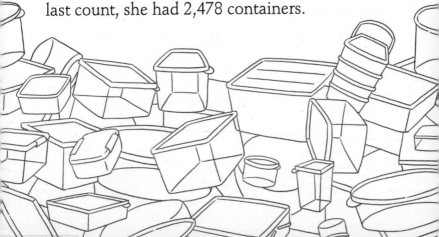

I have no idea what she does with it all but judging by the bruises I got last time I stayed, I swore my bed was made of several dozen of them sellotaped together. Anyway, my **Easter** holidays were dire enough without having to endure being shown her latest set of vacuum seal lids, so I replied, 'No way am I going to Aunt Pat's.'

'I'm staying at Gav's,' Jack repeated.

'WHAT ABOUT ME?' blubbed Oli.

'OK, so *not* Aunt Pat's then,' said Mam, rolling her eyes.

I think our parents felt bad about trying to palm us off onto the most tedious relative in the known universe because afterwards Dad went to the **BAMBOO GARDEN** Chinese takeaway, which is owned by Agung's second cousins, the Chans, to get our tea. Normally we only  go once a month as it is considered a rare treat, like lighting a scented candle, or using a hot water bottle before December. But this was the second time in a week, after last Friday when Dad treated us to the *Special Banquet* with his work bonus.

When he got back from the takeaway, he had some great news. I was hoping he'd splashed out on an extra portion of **prawns on toast**, but it turned out to be even better.

'So, the Chans have a regular customer who runs a bed and breakfast in Sudmouth,' he said.

My ears pricked up. Sudmouth? **THE MEGA BEAST** Sudmouth?

'They were offered a free stay at **Easter** but don't have time to go, so after I told them about the carpet fitting situation, they suggested you kids go instead.'

I did an undetectable air punch and screamed a silent **'YEESSS!!!'**

'One problem though,' said Mam.

Problem? What problem?

'Me and your dad need to stay at home, so who's going to supervise the kids?'

I chipped in quickly, 'Jack's old enough to look after us.'

Nice and crusty

Jack glowered at me. **'Like I said before, I'm staying at Gav's!'**

He has been in a mood with me all week since I told him that the spots on his forehead resembled the shape of a croissant. It was just an amusing observation, but he has been gelling his fringe down in an attempt to hide it.

'Hey, Jack, did you know the sea air has remarkable pimple-removing properties?' I said, hoping to redeem myself.

He sneered and replied, 'I'd rather have a face like **FLAKY PASTRY** for the rest of my life than look after you and Oli for a single day.'

Well I hope his **WILDEST** dream comes true. Then I had a **CRAZY** thought.

'What about Agung?' I suggested. 'He's capable of . . . "supervising".'

We all turned to look at Agung, who was nibbling on a plastic sauce pot lid, having mistaken it for a prawn cracker.

He wasn't helping my case much, and I wish he would remember to put his **blasted** specs on! I should have used some of that flour and water to glue them to his face.

Then I **REMEMBERED** something.

'Wasn't Agung a farmer in Hong Kong when he was a lad?' I said.

'Hard to believe now, but yes, he was,' chuckled Dad.

'Well, you need some **serious** skills to herd cows. And if he could do that, he'll have no problem with us lot.'

Mam and Dad digested this suggestion in

total silence. It was either that or they were digesting the **BURNING** hot bird's eye chillies Mr Chan had hidden in the Szechuan chicken.

I needed an answer quickly so I blurted out in desperation, 'I've looked at the bus timetable and I know which one to catch. Sudmouth's an hour away and it's tiny so we won't get lost, it takes ten minutes to walk from one end to the other.'

Or ten *hours* in Agung's case.

'How come you've looked at the bus timetable already?' said Dad.

I came clean and told him how me and Dev had been devising ways to get on **THE MEGA BEAST**.

64

Then Oli piped up, 'Please can we go on holiday? We haven't been on one for aaaages.'

He was about to turn on the waterworks when our parents finally caved in. For once, Oli's **WHINING** had paid off. Good work, annoying little brother!

'Oh, go on then,' said Dad.

'We don't have a choice really, with the inspectors coming and all,' said Mam. 'But you and Agung need to keep your phones on at all times, do you hear me, Maddy?'

'Cool! Can Dev take Jack's place?' I said, hoping I wasn't going to blow it with another **cheeky request**.

'You need to ask his parents,' said Dad.

GASP! All the things I'd hoped for were coming true!

After tea I dashed over to Dev's to give him the news that was more monumental than the time I completed a Rubik's cube in under five minutes. But first I had to own up about our **Easter** eggs.

'Sorry, Dev, promise to pay you back next year,' I said.

'Never mind that,' he said. 'It's about time your parents got rid of that disgusting blue carpet!'

'Anyway, I am about to impart some information that will **blow** your tiny little mind,' I announced, hardly believing it myself still.

I told him about the trip to Sudmouth, and how he was allowed to take Jack's place.

'**WHAAAT?** We're going to Sudmouth? To go on **THE MEGA BEAST?!**' Dev squealed.

'Yes, but only if your parents say you can,' I said, giving him my you-better-make-it-happen stare.

'Don't worry,' he said. 'I haven't spent six years at drama club for nothing.' Then he stampeded downstairs and dazzled them both with his **Oscar-winning performance**.

How To Be An Amazing Actor

'Yes, of course you can go,' said Mrs Sharma. 'But stay away from the sea because it will give you arthritis.'

Then Mr Sharma added, 'Your grandfather is a well-respected man of the town, Maddy, and I am confident that Dev will be safe in his care.'

I am not sure where he got that impression from, but I wasn't about to put him right.

MEGA BEAST

HERE WE

COME!!!!

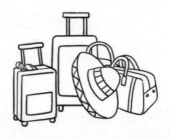

Friday

I was really looking forward to going to Sudmouth today until I woke up this morning and it hit me. Agung wouldn't be supervising us, it'd be more like **us** supervising **him**! He couldn't supervise putting on a pair of matching socks, so how did I ever get my parents to agree to that? They *must* have been **DESPERATE**. I was sure Agung would be all right as long as we kept a close eye on him. Fingers crossed he wouldn't get swallowed up by a freak tidal wave, or whisked off by a **MONSTROUS** albatross, or whatever other dangers lurk at seaside destinations.

How to avoid seaside dangers

Nice

Avoid freak waves by admiring sea from very, very far away

Glue knitting needles to swimming cap as albatross deterrent

Attach drip tray to ice cream to prevent sticky mess

Tape plastic bags around feet to stop sandy toe chafage

Dev called round at eight o'clock. I was almost **blinded** by his yellow Hawaiian shirt with orange palm trees on it. It was a little optimistic considering it was April shower season and the rest of us were wearing cagoules. He did have a sombrero the size of a small satellite dish though, so that would keep him sufficiently dry if it did rain.

'Why have you got two bags?' I asked him.

'Spring wardrobe,' he said, pointing to one. 'And neckerchiefs,' he added, pointing to the other.

AMAZING.

Before we left the house, Mam gave us our

spending money. Oli got extra because it was his birthday last week. I noticed he'd packed his four **Easter** eggs plus the three I'd bribed him with to stop him telling on me when the carpet got ruined. If we're nice to him, maybe the greedy gannet might even part with some.

Then Mam went through the checklist for the **seven hundred billionth** time. Oli asked if he could take Hulk, his school guinea pig.

'That's ridiculous,' said Mam.

She had packed us an ear thermometer, which is **more ridiculous**, if you ask me! Once she was happy we were covered for every emergency, she drove us to the bus stop in the square and dropped us off.

'Call me when you get there,' she said, waving and driving off eagerly.

I knew she was excited about getting the new carpet fitted but she could have at least pretended she was going to miss us, the **COLD-HEARTED WOMAN**!

We sat downstairs on the bus where Agung got a priority seat and a good view.

'What do you reckon the bed and breakfast will be like?' I said to Dev, as the bus rumbled off.

'One of those **boutique** ones with tulle curtains and brass taps,' he answered, dreamily.

'What do you reckon, Oli?' I said.

'I bet it's dead **futuristic** with buttons you can press to get space food delivered by a space cadet,' said Oli.

Oli's a space cadet.

Even I didn't know what the **B&B** was going to be like as I hadn't been told and hadn't thought to ask. I was too preoccupied with the fact I was going on holiday and getting to ride **THE MEGA BEAST**!

We knew we were getting close to Sudmouth when the shop windows started filling up with typical seaside souvenirs like driftwood napkin dispensers and hanging fish mobiles made out of soup cans. No doubt they were aimed at the same numpties that shopped at the ornament section of the garden centre.

The bus terminated at the prom. I know it is only a load of murky, **FREEZING COLD WATER** but I will never get over how magical it is to see the sea!

The **B&B** was two minutes' walk away. I found the decor inside *interesting*. They had managed to replicate the dated **1970s** look quite well, in a modern retro way. Agung stroked the burgundy velvet flocked wallpaper and said, 'hao liang' which I know means 'very nice', so it got his seal of approval.

An oldish lady with bright pink lipstick appeared in reception.

'Hello, dears, can I help you?' she said.

I answered, 'We're the Yips.'

'Oh yes, we've been expecting you . . .

DEREEEK!'

she screeched.

A man came out of the kitchen, drying his hands on an I ♥ *Sudmouth* tea towel.

'I'm Wendy and this is my husband, Derek,' she said.

A **gigantic** St Bernard lolloped towards us.

'And this is **Princess**!'

The half-tonne hound immediately jumped on Oli, who toppled backwards and got trapped underneath.

'PRINCESS, GET OFF!' Derek shouted.

Me and Dev tried not to laugh as we pulled Oli up off the floor. I couldn't tell if he was crying as his face was soaked in drool.

After apologising and drying Oli off with his tea towel, Derek showed us to our rooms. (Me and Dev in one, Agung and Oli in the other). I noticed the seventies theme continued upstairs. While Agung and Oli unpacked in their room, I had a look around ours but stopped to gobble the **complimentary shortbread**. My joy was short lived when I opened the wardrobe door and the knob came off in my hand. It turned out the seventies look wasn't retro at all because in actual fact, none of the furnishings had been updated for **five decades!**

FANTASTIC.

'Maybe we'll get lucky with a breath-taking view of the ocean?' I said to Dev, pulling the net curtains to one side.

I looked out of the window and was delighted to see . . . nothing but the local cockle stand in the public car park. **OH**.

'What about the bathroom? You might find something marvellous in there,' said Dev.

I stuck my head around the door and indeed I did find something marvellous. **Marvellously frightful!** I didn't even know bathroom suites came in mushy pea green, or that it was even legal! I did find some nice mini bottles of shampoo and conditioner though, which I planned to wrap as Christmas presents for Mam.

'THERE'S TWO LOOS IN HERE!'

shouted Oli, from his bathroom next door.

I went to see what nonsense he was spouting and had to correct him, as one of the loos was actually a bidet. I only know because I saw one once on a house renovation programme Agung was watching. We can't do chatting so instead we laugh and shout at the telly together.

'What's a bidet?' Oli asked.

I tried to put it the best way
I could.

'It's a hygiene device designed to keep the "downstairs" areas clean,' I said.

'So why is it *upstairs* in here, then?' he said.

LORD SAVE ME.

It was two o'clock by the time we'd finished faffing about. It didn't help that it took Dev ages unpacking and refolding his neckerchiefs. Then, just as I thought he was done, he pulled out a pair of **slip-on roller skates** and started polishing them!

'Just in case there's a roller disco nearby,' he explained.

I didn't want to call Mam as we were about

to head out to the fish and chip shop and she is prone to verbal diarrhoea so I texted her instead, to tell her we'd arrived safely.

Agung had never tried a **pickled egg** before so I bought one for him as an alternative **Easter** egg treat. If there are two things that should never be allowed to go together, they would be eggs and vinegar. (Also, flour and water, if you include the disaster earlier in the week). Agung would seem to disagree though, as he wolfed the **STINKY** thing down in one go and did a little bum parp in appreciation.

Afterwards we wandered along the high street where I got lemon sherbets for Agung, a stick of rock for me and Dev, fizz bombs for Oli and fudge for Dad. Mam doesn't eat sweets but I didn't want her to get left out. I decided that if I went past a health food shop I would be a thoughtful daughter and get her a kilo of dried lentils. Then it was time for the most momentous part of the trip so far – buying our Mega Beast tickets at the amusement park by the seafront. Up until then Oli hadn't expressed any interest

about going on, but when he saw the top of the ride over the perimeter fence, he looked as if a tribe of ewoks from the forest moon of Endor had suddenly materialised before him.

'Three tickets for **THE MEGA BEAST** please!' I chirped, when I got to the ticket booth.

SUDMOUTH
AMUSEMENT PARK

'Got your vouchers?' said the lad in the booth.

'What vouchers?' I said, my jaw dropping.

'Yeah, what vouchers?' said Dev.

The lad sighed heavily: 'You need special vouchers for the opening week of the ride, because it's so busy and we have to manage the queues.'

BRILLIANT.

'Nobody told us about vouchers. It's not on the posters or anything!' I said, trying not to sound too hysterical.

The lad shrugged. 'Don't shoot the messenger.'

'Where do we get these vouchers from?' said Dev, panicking just as much as I was.

'They're in the **Sudmouth Post** all week,' said the lad.

Then he craned his neck and shouted **'NEXT!'** to the people waiting behind us. How rude.

It was probably easy enough to get hold of the vouchers, but it meant we couldn't get our tickets till the next day – **WHAT A PAIN!** There was only one thing for it. We would have to make sure we got to the newsagent's bright and early the next morning.

Saturday - first thing

Dev's **thunderous** snoring woke me at two a.m. then an *angry* seagull woke me at a quarter to six! I got up to **bang** on the window and scare it off, but when I drew back the curtains, the bird was **GINORMOUS**. It had a pair of mangled spectacles in its beak. I am sure it was one of those **MONSTROUS** killer albatrosses I've heard about and it had obviously just taken a victim.

I quickly drew the curtains closed again and jumped back into bed in shock. I took ages to nod off, then Dev prodded me awake at eight, which was way later than planned.

Dev was already washed and dressed, in *gold* jogging bottoms and a **TIGER PRINT** fleece. He wore that outfit in Plunkthorpe once and an old lady asked if the circus was in town.

'Did you hear that mad seagull this morning?' I asked.

'No, but I heard you mumbling in your sleep about not wanting your eyes pecked out,' said Dev.

'Well, FYI you snore like a hippo face down

in a vat of jelly,' I said.

'It's not my fault, it's these pillows,' said Dev. 'The polyester stuffing swells my sinuses.'

I dressed and rushed downstairs, hoping the newsagent's hadn't sold out of **Sudmouth Posts**. We needed to get hold of those vouchers so we could get on the ride – it was the whole point of being here. Oli and Agung were already having breakfast in the dining room.

'Look, Maddy, mini marmalade!' said Oli, presenting me with a dish of assorted preserves in tiny little jars.

He knew that trying a mini marmalade was on my list of things to do before I turned into a boring old adult with no sense of adventure. It changed from week to week but at the moment my list looked like this:

5) Try a mini marmalade to see if tastes any different from regular-sized marmalade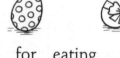

4) Knit a gilet made out of wool woven from **FUZZFACE**'s moulted fur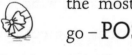

3) Break Plunkthorpe record for eating the most chocolate Easter eggs in one go – POSTPONED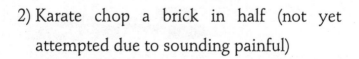

2) Karate chop a brick in half (not yet attempted due to sounding painful)

1) Get my own room (this has occupied top
   spot since Oli's birth)

Unfortunately I had more urgent matters to
attend to. 'Oli, stay here and watch Agung. Me
and Dev are off to the newsagent's. We'll be
back in ten minutes,' I said.

We were just about to go forth on our urgent
quest when my mobile phone rang. It was Mam.

GREAT.

She always calls at the most inconvenient
moments and it is normally about nothing
in particular. From what I've gathered over
the years though, it's a trait that all mams
share.

'Hiya, Mam,' I said, slightly irked.

'Hiya, Maddy!' said Mam. 'Did you get there all right?'

She was only one question in and the conversation was already nonsensical. Of course I got there all right, I texted to tell her that yesterday! Although any normal mam would have called to ask as soon as we'd arrived. Knowing her, she was probably preoccupied admiring the new carpet.

'YEEEES.'

'What's the **B&B** like then?' she asked.

This really was NOT the time for unnecessary

chit chat. I had important things to get on with.

'**Top notch** establishment!' I said, doing complete Dev acting.

'Have you had brekkie?'

'Not yet, but . . .'

'Make sure you have brekkie, it's *free*!' she said. 'And don't forget to eat some wholegrains. You don't want to get bunged up.'

'Mam, can we leave the subject of my **bowel movements** for another time please?'

Dev punched my arm, jabbed his watch and clenched his teeth at me. Translated into words

I knew that meant, **'STOP BEING A DORK, HANG UP NOW AND BE PRONTO ABOUT IT!'**

I couldn't get a word in edgeways though, as Mam was busy updating me on the carpet situation with a detailed account of sub-floor preparation.

I nodded and muttered, 'Nail gun? Fabulous. Stanley knife? Lovely.'

Then Dev **kicked** me in the shin. It was fairly painful so I am sure he took the top layer of skin off.

'**OW!** Listen. Mam, can I call you later? It's just that . . .'

I looked at Oli who was shaking Luke violently upside down. For some unknown reason he had inserted Luke's head into one of the empty preserve jars and it was stuck tight.

'. . . Luke's got jammed in the jam,' I bumbled.

'Eh?' said Mam.

'Bye,' I said briskly, and hung up before she could come up with any more inane **nonsense** that would delay us even further.

Me and Dev were about to make our way out when Derek came over to the table. He said **nicely**, 'Sorry to ask but there's some other guests waiting for this table. Are your brother and grandad finished yet? They've been here since dawn.'

'Who's Dawn?' said Oli.

I apologised to Derek (for Oli's ditsy remark as well as for them **hogging** the breakfast table) and told Oli to take Agung back to their room. He kicked up a **fuss** and **demanded** to come with us. To make things worse, he wouldn't leave the **B&B** until the jar had been removed from the stupid doll's head. Derek asked if he could help. We showed him the problem and he whistled *Princess* over. He held the doll to the huge hound's mouth and she started licking it all over – **gross!** After a few seconds Derek took hold of the jar and twisted it off, just like that! It turns out dog slobber has its positives after all.

Practical uses for dog slobber

Loosening dolls' heads from mini jam jars

Plunk!

Everlasting envelope licker

Cooool!

Excellent water slide slimer

Playing a GENIUS joke on Jack

heh heh

HAIR GEL

Once Oli was happy, we exited the building and I was surprised to find it was not pitch black outside as I had expected. We had been held up with one thing or another for so long I thought it might have been night time already. There were more delays when Agung decided to pop into a hardware shop to test the bristle stiffness on the yard brushes. For someone who is so easily distracted, it is a wonder how he had ever become a **cow herder**. Perhaps he only had one cow!

At one point I turned around to check on him and he had disappeared. I had horrible visions of him flying halfway to the Netherlands in the clutches of a **monster** seabird when someone shouted out, 'Excuse me, does this gentleman belong with you?' It was the owner of the chip shop we went to yesterday standing on his doorstep with Agung.

'I think he wants a **pickled egg**,' said the shop owner.

'**Yeah!**' said Agung, nodding avidly.

He'd just had his breakfast, for crying out loud! I bought him one then we set off again, but this time I kept a firm hold of Agung's arm. I wish I didn't have to as he kept dribbling **pickled egg** juice down my left sleeve all the way down the street, but at least he couldn't wander off. Finally we reached the newsagent's and when I saw the sign I laughed out loud.

'Look, it's called MacCavity's,' I announced, to everyone.

'And?' said Dev, looking at me weirdly.

'Well, wouldn't that be a brilliant name for a dentist, if his first name was *Phil*? You know, Phil MacCavity. **HAHAHA!**'

No one found it funny except me.

'I think you might be sleep deprived,' said Dev, sympathetically. 'Let's get these newspapers, then you can go back to the **B&B** for a nice little nap.'

The joke was on me in the end as MacCavity's had just sold the last copy of today's **Sudmouth Post**! The next paper shop we went to was sold out too.

FANTASTIC.

It must have been karma. I was being punished for the carpet-wrecking incident.

After visiting every paper shop in town and despairing as each one informed us they had sold out, I felt like sitting in a dark room and listening to sad violin tunes on maximum volume for all eternity.

'We will **NOT** depart Sudmouth without going on **THE MEGA BEAST**!' snapped Dev, flicking his head back and thrusting his hands on his hips.

HE IS SUCH A DRAMA QUEEN.

'I'll tell Mam on you if you don't make it happen!' snivelled Oli.

'I want eat more pickle egg,' said Agung, punctuating the end of the sentence with a **BOTTOM BURP.**

For all the above reasons, I was now declaring this a state of emergency.

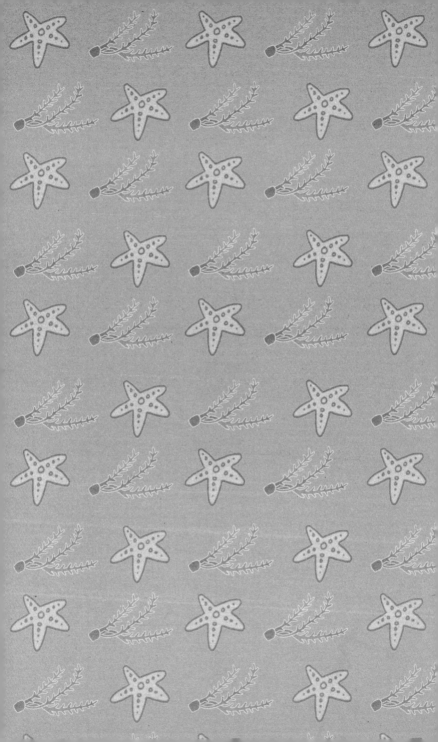

Saturday morning

Don't ask me why but I made everyone walk to the amusement park so I could torture myself by staring longingly at **THE MEGA BEAST** through the railings. The queue was already a mile long. No wonder all the **Sudmouth Posts** were sold out. Those people must have camped outside the paper shops overnight to get their vouchers in time. Wish I had thought of that. I still have much to learn in this cruel world.

'I WANNA GO ON THAT!' said Oli, pointing at the kiddie's land train rumbling past.

I sighed heavily and replied, 'We might have to make do with that if things carry on the way they are.'

'Actually, if the driver put his foot down over a few speed bumps, it would make a good substitute for **THE MEGA BEAST**,' said Dev, ever the annoying optimist.

I couldn't think what else to do except go back to the **B&B**, stare at the peeling wallpaper then sob into my polyester-stuffed pillow.

'We must not be defeated!' cried Dev, shaking me out of my pitiful state.

'Luke'll help us look for vouchers. He's the greatest **Jedi** the galaxy has ever known,' said Oli, making Luke's eyes rotate from side to side.

Agung patted me encouragingly on the back and kindly offered me a sherbet lemon with bits of fluff stuck to it out of his cagoule pocket.

They were **right**. We didn't come all this way for nothing.

'OK, what other places will have newspapers?' I said.

'Erm, hairdressers . . . or a library?' said Oli.

For someone who sticks dolls' heads in jam

jars, he is not as daft as he looks.

'Good call, Oli,' I said. 'We went past a hairdresser's in the high street earlier. I remember because Dev said his next hairdo would be a pink pixie bob like the model on the poster.'

'Purple,' said Dev, correcting me.

'Pink, purple, polka dot. This is no time for splitting hairs (har har). We need to get moving now!' I said, ushering them back towards the high street.

When we got there, we glanced through the open door.

'Look, that lady's got our paper!' said Oli.

Sure enough, underneath a dryer was a withered old woman with a foil-covered head reading the **Sudmouth Post**. She looked like she'd been left there and been forgotten about since dinosaurs roamed the earth.

'How do we get hold of it?' Dev whispered.

'We could wait until she's completely mummified. Could be quite soon by the looks of it,' I smirked.

Dev snorted, 'Or I could get a stink bomb from that joke shop across the road and set it off inside the salon.'

'Why use a stink bomb when we've got Agung?' I said.

Agung responded accordingly with a loud **TRUMP**. He has been suffering such atrocious wind since he started on those **WHIFFY pickled eggs** that I might have to ban him from eating them. The blast of passing wind must have startled one of the stylists because he came out and said stiffly, 'Can I help at all?'

I asked if he had any spare copies of the **Sudmouth Post** and he replied, 'Only for paying customers.' I wanted to alert him about the old woman being fossilised under the dryer, but he clearly did not want to engage in any more conversation, so we left.

Undeterred, we carried on to our next destination, the **library**. You can always find helpful friendly people in libraries so we were sure to get some answers there.

Outside was a banner with *Sudmouth Entomologists' Society Family Fun Day* on it and underneath, the caption *Bee there or bee square!*

SUDMOUTH ENTOMOLOGISTS' SOCIETY FAMILY FUN DAY
"BEE THERE OR BEE SQUARE"

'What's an *En-too-moo-log-gisks?*' Oli asked.

'I don't know. But I know what an *Entomologist* is. They study insects.'

Then Dev jumped in and said, 'Hey, what goes ninety-nine thump, ninety-nine thump?'

'What?' I replied.

'A centipede with a wooden leg!'

Oli **laughed** so hard he started **choking**, until a lady in a stag beetle costume saved him with a cup of squash (as a drink, not throwing it over his head like I would have done). I thought it was ever so **kind** of her, until it became evident that she wanted us to fill in a twenty-seven-page questionnaire about the loss of wild habitats. She ought to come round to our house, then she'd find that wild habitats were actually thriving – **HA!** We politely passed on the questionnaire, as time was ticking on.

In the main room, experts were showcasing different **critters**. Before I could stop him, Oli rushed over to see the man with the **tarantula**, or 'Spider-Man' as I quite wittily remarked to Dev. But when I turned around, Dev wasn't there. He was **COWERING** on top of a stool in the self-help section. I had forgotten about his morbid fear of **spiders**. I found a thick hardback about overcoming arachnophobia and handed it to him.

'I haven't got time to read all that,' he said.

'No, you use it to bash the spider with,' I quipped. 'Now keep an eye on Agung and Oli while I go and check the newspaper section.'

I couldn't believe it, but every paper was there *except* the flipping **Sudmouth Post**!

When I went back to find the others they had moved on to the cockroach expert. To my horror, cockroach woman plucked one of the revolting creatures out of the tank and passed it around for the audience to hold. Was the library supervisor aware of this deranged lady? Oli was right at the front as well. Mam would kill me if he ended up contracting a **DEADLY DISEASE** from an insect that could suck your brains out with their secret chin tusks (or maybe I am getting them mixed up with Chihuahuas?) I pushed my way over to rescue Oli from certain doom when something caught my eye. The bottom of the tank was lined with none other than today's **Sudmouth Post**! I could actually see the voucher! How could I get to it though? Several ideas popped into my head:

a) Utilise Agung, the human stink bomb

b) Accidentally on purpose trip up and knock the tank over, thereby causing enough mayhem for me to retrieve the paper without anyone noticing

c) Straight up look like a weirdo and ask if I can have it

How to obtain a precious voucher

Use human stink bomb to clear the room

PARPITY PARP!

Distract by falling over everything

Distract by pretending to be chased by a chin-tusked Chihuahua

Just ASK FOR IT (even if it IS covered in insect poo!)

VOUCHER

I was about to opt for c) when upon closer inspection, I noticed that the newspaper was covered in droppings.

YUCK!

I wasn't about to stoop that low. She could keep that **filthy** bit of paper for her **filthy** insects. It made me feel quite faint until I realised the queasiness was due to missing breakfast.

I gathered everyone together and we left to get some food.

We found a café next to the beach with an excellent window table looking out to sea. How nice it was to relax and not have to worry about those blasted vouchers for a while.

Unfortunately that niceness only lasted a fraction of a millisecond because while we were waiting for the server to come over with the menus, something fluttered past outside.

'SEE THAT?' I cried.

'What?' said Dev.

'That was a **Sudmouth Post**! Stay here!' I said to Oli and Agung.

Me and Dev darted outside to pursue it. We tried to keep up as it tumbled along the prom but we had to stop several times. Me to stop for breath, and Dev to stop for breath and fix his hair. Luckily the paper got caught on a stack of deckchairs. Dev lunged for it but he missed and it blew off again. His faux fur bag's pompom got caught on a chair leg and I told him to leave it. He said it was limited edition and DEBONY DELITE from *Girlzlife* had the same one. By the time he'd finished telling me that **incredible** piece of celebrity gossip, the newspaper had whisked onto the beach. I wish it hadn't as the one thing that annoys me more than Ted and Tod is sand in between my toes. It gives me horrendous chafing. **But I needed the voucher!** I mustered up the courage for one last dash onto the beach, hopefully without tripping over a giant conch and drowning in the sea. The paper got stuck on some seaweed. As I grabbed it a wave came and soaked me from the knees down. According to Mrs Sharma I was bound to get arthritis now.

Dev stumbled over ungraciously.

'HHHUNNNNGHH,' he gasped.

123

'What was that?' I said.

'My . . . my . . . huuunngggh,' he wheezed, pointing to his bag.

I realised he needed his inhaler so fetched it out of his bag for him. He had a few puffs and collapsed in an ugly heap next to me.

GASP!

We might have been completely battered by that unexpected nautical-themed obstacle course, but at least the newspaper was in one piece! It was however, completely drenched, so it was of utmost urgency that we all headed back to the B&B where I could save it with a hairdryer.

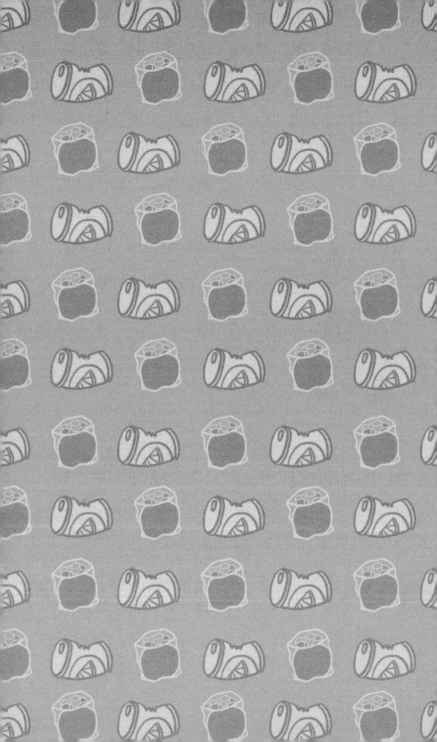

Saturday afternoon

There was moaning all the way back to the **B&B** about missing lunch at the café. I said to Agung, 'Tell you what, I'll make you your favourite instant cup noodle with a pickled egg on top.'

He definitely knew those English words because he clapped and shouted, **'Hao liang!'**

'What about me?' said Oli.

'You can have the biggest gobstopper I can find,' I said.

I carefully dried and cut out the voucher, put it in an envelope I found in the bedside drawer and locked it firmly in the safe like gold bullion. Afterwards I tried drying my trousers with the hairdryer too, but the motor had worn out and wouldn't have dried a combover on an ant.

What to do with a pathetic hairdryer

Dry combover on an ant ✗

Store it somewhere important, for example...

THE BIN! ✓

I didn't think I'd end up in the sea fully dressed (not a typical holiday pastime – unless you're Victorian), so I'd only brought one pair of trousers with me. Dev offered to lend me a pair from his extensive spring wardrobe, but the only choices were:

a) Paisley harem pants

b) Turquoise velvet jeggings

c) The gold jogging bottoms he had on today (These were soggy so I couldn't wear them.)

I would rather have worn a bin bag than go out looking like a fan of **DEBONY DELITE** from *Girlzlife*, so I insisted that he give me the more acceptable camouflage cargo pants he'd brought along as spare emergency back-ups, and he wear a) or b) instead.

Just as I thought my day was improving slightly, Oli whined, **'I'M HUNGRRRRY.'** Honestly, since when was staying alive more important than getting on **THE MEGA BEAST**?! That boy needs to take a long hard look at himself and get his priorities straight. Mind you, we had missed lunch and it was almost half two. Feeding him would be far more favourable than adding Social Services onto my list of nightmare scenarios.

On the way out Wendy caught us at reception. **ARGH!** This holiday was one hold up after another.

'Afternoon, everyone. Lovely day for it,' she said.

If she meant lovely day for running around, getting stressed and going slowly mad then she was spot on.

'Have you been anywhere nice so far?' she asked.

'We saw cockroaches in the library!' said Oli.

Wendy frowned. 'Well, I'm sorry about that. I hope you've reported it to Sudmouth Council's pest control office.'

I couldn't be bothered to explain that that's not what Oli meant.

'And we haven't had lunch yet!' Oli sniffed.

What. A. Blabbermouth.

'Aw, look at him, scrawny little thing,' Wendy cooed. 'I'll make you lunch on the house if you like. Mr and Mrs Chan are always giving us free spring rolls, so it's the least I can do.'

'That would be awesome, thanks, Wendy,' I said, brightening up.

To be honest, I couldn't face going out again yet. It would take at least five nights of lying on the couch, watching telly and stuffing my face with *CROCODILE CRUNCHIES* to recover from that horrific ordeal on the beach earlier. My underdeveloped fibulas just aren't built to handle that kind of activity.

Wendy sat us down at a table while she went to sort out our food.

'Is Wendy up on the roof?' asked Oli, wide-eyed in wonder.

'What are you on about?' I said.

'She said she was going to make us something "On the house", so she must be on the roof,' he pondered.

AMAZING.

Twenty minutes later Wendy wafted in with four plates of baked beans and mash. Unfortunately Agung ended up with one of the mash lumps on his lap after it slid off his plate due to the table being wobbly.

Wendy wedged some paper underneath the offending leg and made some fresh mash for Agung.

After everyone was fed and watered, we ventured out again in pursuit of the elusive **Sudmouth Post**. I felt like I was dressed for the part in my **camouflage gear**. I couldn't say Dev felt the same in the paisley harem pants he'd changed into after his jogging bottoms got covered in wet sand.

We decided to try the park this time, hoping that someone would have left a copy on a bench somewhere. Me and Dev wanted to do a quick scour of the grounds, but it meant leaving Agung and Oli on their own and that was not an option. I spotted a man by the fountain selling novelty helium balloons and got an idea.

'Hey, Dev, what about I get a couple of those balloons and tie them to Agung and Oli. That way we can keep an eye on them from wherever we are in the park.'

Dev glared at me and uttered, **'That's *outrageous!'***

From his reaction, I thought I'd gone too far this time and replied, 'Yes, you're right. It is irresponsible to treat my nearest and dearest like circus animals – even if they do act like them most of the time.'

Then Dev cackled, 'Don't be daft, **I LOVE IT**!'

I should have known that Dev would go for anything outrageous.

'Brill, then let's do it,' I said.

I couldn't find a **Star Wars** themed

balloon, so I got Oli a *JEFFREY THE JUMBO JET* one instead. It was the nearest thing I could find to the **Millennium Falcon**. I bought Agung the biggest brightest one, which happened to be *Magic Moo* from the My Mini Cow family. There was no way we could lose them now and even if we did, all we'd have to do is tell the police to search for two daft juvenile characters hanging about town.

The vendor put extra string on the balloons like I asked, so they could float high enough to see from a fair distance, and there was enough left to tie around Agung and Oli's waists.

Surprisingly they didn't object like I was expecting them to, but that's because they had their gobs full of Mr Whippy ice cream with double flakes and extra sprinkles that I had bought specifically for that purpose.

There weren't any copies of the **Sudmouth Post** on the benches, so our search extended into the bushes. There was nothing except stinging nettles and scratchy twigs that got caught on everything. I was wondering if we should have been wandering about in such treacherous territory when a ball came flying from nowhere and hit me straight in the eye. Then some kind of **MONSTROUS** yeti bowled into me and knocked me flat on my back.

'YOU ALL RIGHT?' a voice said.

It was Derek. He was out walking *Princess*. He apologised and helped me up. 'Fancy seeing you here.'

He gave me and Dev a puzzled look.

'Oh, we've volunteered to do a litter pick,' Dev panted, jogging over.

'That's good of you,' said Derek.

HA! As if!

I suspected Derek was about to embark on a long and laborious tale about something completely irrelevant. Then sure enough . . .

'Did you know, I've been going to the **BAMBOO GARDEN** takeaway for my birthday since nineteen eighty-five?'

GREAT.

'No, no I didn't,' I said, failing to do interested acting.

'We get the same dishes every time: chicken chop suey, beef curry, sweet and sour pork and special fried rice . . . since nineteen eighty-five,' he said, triumphantly.

What did he want, a **FLIPPING MEDAL?!**

'The sweet and sour pork's for our *Princess*. She loves Chinese food. But do you know what her most favourite treat is?'

Illuminate us, Derek.

'She's obsessed with anything sweet!'

There was a distant bark. While Derek was wittering on, *Princess* had roamed off on her extendable lead and was digging out the contents of a bin.

'NAUGHTY PRINCESS!' Derek shouted, rushing over to pull a half-eaten corn on the cob out of her mouth.

We wandered over to eyeball the mess she'd made.

'Sorry, just as you'd tidied up so nicely as well!' said Derek.

'Not to worry, we'll clear this up,' said Dev.

I thought Dev sounded strangely enthusiastic until he elbowed me in the ribs and held something up to show me. It was a copy of the **Sudmouth Post** he'd found in the pile of rubbish! **WOO-HOO!**

We couldn't help but hop about with utter joy among the rotten banana skins and mouldy crumpled juice cartons. I bet Derek was wondering how on earth litter picking could be so **exhilarating!**

When Agung ambled over to see what the fuss was about, Derek took one look at *Magic Moo* strapped to him, made his excuses and hurried off with *Princess*, which wasn't easy as she was straining on the lead like an ox trying to nab Agung's ice cream.

When we got back to the **B&B** the first thing I did was lock voucher number two up with the first one. I had **five missed calls** from Mam on my phone, but I was too tired to call her back.

ZZ Z^Z ZZ^Z^Z

Sunday morning

ARRRRGGGHH, I overslept!

It was gone ten o'clock by the time I woke up – the day was practically over with! All my plans of getting to **MacCavity's** the second they opened this morning were down the drain. Forget about heading to the newsagent's, the only thing I was heading for was a **nervous breakdown**!

I was so broken from yesterday that I had slept through Dev's deafening snoring and my phone alarm. It was the **squawking** seagull that woke me in the end. I should have been grateful but the thought of a *KILLER BEAST* on our windowsill was scaring me witless. I had to get rid of it. Reluctantly I opened the window and poked at it with a teaspoon. It was the only thing that resembled a weapon close to hand.

How to defend yourself from a killer seagull

Poke at it with a teaspoon

SQUAWK!

Woefully inadequate

✗

Threaten it with a shovel

✓

The gull swiped it and chucked it onto the street below, narrowly missing a postwoman on her bike. Imagine the **CATASTROPHE** if it had landed in her spokes!

Then it spotted the packet of shortbread on the sideboard and tried to barge its way in, and I am not **EXAGGERATING** when I say it had the wingspan of a Boeing 747! I had to wrestle the window shut without losing my fingers and throughout the whole traumatic ordeal, Dev slept like a baby. It is all right for some!

I couldn't believe I had just woken up and already wished I was back in bed. I dreaded what the rest of the day had in store. Dev was in such a deep sleep that I had to resort to **slapping** him on the cheeks.

'What d'you do that for?' he grumbled.

'IT WAS EITHER THAT OR A BOOT UP THE BUTTOCKS,' I replied.

After washing and dressing in record time, we went downstairs (my trousers were still damp so I had to wear Dev's cargo pants again). Agung and Oli had just finished breakfast.

'Why didn't you wake us?' I said to Oli.

'You didn't tell me to,' he said.

EXCELLENT.

'Why didn't you save us any brekkie then?' I asked.

Agung answered with a hearty **BURP**.

Cor, the things I do for these people and *this* is what I get in return!

Oli must have felt unusually guilty, as he sprinted up to his room and returned with two of his bribery **Easter** eggs for our breakfast. I chomped on a bit and nearly gagged. I checked the best before date on the box and discovered they were off. No wonder Oli was so keen to offload them onto us, plus it served us right for scrimping at the **NINETY-NINE PENCE SHOP!**

Anyway, we didn't need breakfast, we needed one more voucher. It was our last day in Sudmouth, the amusement park closed at five and we were due to get the six o'clock bus home. Timings were tight, but we could do it! I rounded everyone up, we made our way to **MacCavity's** and hoped for the best.

When we got there the shopkeeper was arranging coral reef snow globes on the shelf. The souvenirs in this town got more and more **ridiculous**.

'Excuse me, do you have any copies of the *Sudmouth Post* left?' I asked the shopkeeper.

He turned to look at me as if I was an alien and exclaimed, 'The **Sudmouth Post** doesn't come out on Sundays, it's the **Sunday Suds** today!'

'PLEASE KICK ME,' I said to Dev, depressed.

'Only if you kick me first,' said Dev, even more depressed.

'I'll have none of that funny business in here, thank you,' said the shopkeeper.

I don't know what part of that he found funny, because I certainly wasn't laughing.

'Does the **Sunday Suds** have a **MEGA BEAST** voucher in it?' I said.

'A what?' he replied.

FANTASTIC.

A purveyor of news who didn't even know what was going on in his local community. While the shopkeeper continued stacking his summertime snow product, Agung and Oli went to inspect the pick 'n' mix and me and Dev went to check out the **Sunday Suds**. We picked up a copy and immediately saw the headline:

SUNDAY SUDS

UFOS SPOTTED OVER SUDMOUTH!

WHAT?! How come we never saw that? Then I remembered it was because we'd been busy loitering around hair salons, cringing at cockroaches and messing about with stupid novelty balloons all day yesterday. We read the article:

'Yesterday at approximately 5 p.m., dozens of residents in Sudmouth witnessed two unidentified flying objects in the sky directly above Central Gardens. Several photographs were taken of the unexplained aerial observations and sent to the National UFO Research Association for further investigations.'

'Awesomesauceness!' Dev gasped.

There was something weird about the zoomed-in picture. It was blurry but I recognised the faint outlines.

'Hoooold on a minute,' I said.

'What?' said Dev.

'Those aren't UFOs,' I snickered.

'What are they then?'

'They're flipping **JEFFREY THE JUMBO JET** and *Magic Moo*!'

Dev shrieked and the shopkeeper glared at us.

'SHHH!' I giggled. 'This can be our little secret.'

Right then we didn't care if our holiday had been a shambles so far, we'd made the local headline news – **HILARIOUS!**

After a sift through the inside pages, we were disappointed to find that the *Sunday*

Suds didn't contain any vouchers but we bought a couple of copies as souvenirs – miles better than a coral reef snow globe!

Agung treated us each to a bag of **pick 'n' mix,** so we went to the beach to tuck in and formulate another plan. Just as I went to chuck my empty bag in the bin, I had a thought.

'Hey, Dev, are you thinking what I'm thinking?'

'What, that a Chihuahua might burst out and spear you with its chin tusk?'

'Apart from that.'

'Dunno.'

'We found our last voucher in the bin. So maybe there's another in *this* one?'

Dev laughed mockingly and replied, 'I'm not getting my trench coat covered in bin juice. It's dry clean only!'

'OK, I'll do it myself then!' I said.

I don't know what came over me but I rolled up my sleeves, held my breath and dived right into the rancid receptacle. I managed to pull out a broken brolly, a child's sandal and a squashed pineapple before someone shouted out, **'OI!** I could get you fined for **CHUCKING RUBBISH** about!' A warden brandishing a large litter picker marched towards us.

'Sorry, I was trying to find something,' I said, scooping the rubbish back in the bin.

'Are you with a responsible adult?' he asked.

'Yes, over there,' I said, nodding over to Agung, who was in the process of sticking two foam bananas into his mouth like fangs.

The warden tried explaining to Agung the heinous crime that I had just committed and got a **banana fang grin** in response.

When the warden realised he wasn't getting anywhere, he insisted on accompanying us back to the **B&B** so he could report my anti-social behaviour to any available adult with a basic grasp of English. It turned out Wendy and Derek knew him. His name was Keith and he wasn't a litter warden at all, but a local busybody. All Derek had to do was call **Princess** over to slobber over Keith until he pleaded for mercy and ran off.

Wendy brought us a tray of tea and shortbread (they don't offer any other type of biscuit) in the dining room, where we were discussing our next move.

'Don't suppose we'll get the last voucher now. We might as well pack our stuff and go home,' I said.

'No, I wanna go on **THE MEGA BEAST**!' whinged Oli, throwing Luke on the floor in a fit.

I went to pick him up before **Princess** got her slobbery chops on him and as I bent down, I spied something underneath the table leg. It was the wedge of paper Wendy had used to stop it wobbling. In a moment of optimistic madness I slid it out and unravelled it. It was a page out of the **Sudmouth Post** with **THE MEGA BEAST** voucher on it! It had been under our noses the whole time!

Sunday – late morning

WOO-HOO! We had all three vouchers at last! After a blissful second of letting it sink in, we had a maniacal five-minute victory conga around the dining room of the **B&B.** Everyone except Agung, that is, who claimed his sciatica was playing up but really he was too busy scoffing the complimentary shortbread. Even **Princess** joined in bounding around, until her delicate ankles gave way under her colossal body weight and she toppled into the

163

crockery cabinet. Wendy reassured us that there was no damage as even though **Princess** was built like a World War Two tank, all the decorative crockery on the premises was glued down due to her clumsiness (**Princess**'s not Wendy's).

I sprang upstairs, fetched the other vouchers and hustled everyone out of the door. We were so excited. The whole reason we were in Sudmouth was about to happen!

There was a longish queue at the ticket booth but for once we had plenty of time. The park wasn't closing for another four hours so we could take it easy. It was difficult though. No matter how hard I conjured up calming images of wicker baskets full of baby sloths in tutus, I could not relax.

Baby sloth in a tutu

Gerbil in an egg cup

Duckling in a daisy hat

Panda in pants

It had been one disaster after another since we arrived, so why shouldn't anything else go wrong at any minute? I took a deep breath and hummed, **'OMMMM'**, like Mam does every time an electric bill comes through the door. But then Oli swatted me with his doll.

165

'What did you do that for?' I said.

'I thought that humming sound was a wasp!' he said.

So much for that calming technique.

The queue was getting shorter. We were nearly there. **THE MEGA BEAST** was within our grasp! Just then I saw something that made my stomach lurch. It wasn't the pigeon pecking at the squashed kebab on the tarmac, or Oli picking his nose and eating it. It was **GED SPONGER**, the **BULLY**, from school! He was by the waffle stand with an old lady in a woollen waistcoat. I knew it was his granny because Ged visited her at the Autumnal Leaves care home's open evening when I helped out on the cake stall. They must have been on a day trip. Nice for them, but hell on earth for me.

'Dev, don't look now, but Ged Sponger's in town getting a *toffee sauce tower*!' I whispered loudly.

Immediately Dev did a most obvious three-hundred-and-sixty-degree pirouette with a bobbing meerkat head movement. Subtlety has never been his strong point.

'Oh my god, Ged Sponger's in town getting a toffee sauce tower!' he hissed.

Dev also likes repeating what you've said, while adding his own theatrical twist for effect.

It is very irritating. I didn't want Ged to see us. He still hadn't got me and Dev back for making him fall into the care home's ornamental fish pond. I swore it was an accident! We were meant to catch Oli's runaway guinea pig, but due to my uncoordinated upper limbs and Dev's useless aim, we chucked the tablecloth/net over Ged's hard-to-miss massive bonce by mistake, thereby obscuring his vision and directing him into the huge stagnant puddle – **HA! HA!**

I didn't want to lose our place in the queue but there was no telling what Ged would do if he spotted us. I moved everyone away to hide behind a nearby photo board. A classic one with the skinny man and portly woman in matching one-piece bathing suits painted on it. Once everyone was safely behind, me and Dev stuck

our heads through the face-holes where we could keep an eye on Ged's movements.

It turned out to be quite amusing as it happens. Ged's granny was waving her brolly at a hostile seagull but accidentally whacked Ged over the head instead. Me and Dev tried not to laugh out loud as he rubbed his head, dropped his waffle and the seagull flew off with it. Then his granny pointed at the photo board and they started walking over. **OH NO!** Hopefully he wouldn't recognise us – he is, after all, known as the biggest plonker in Plunkthorpe. I froze my face into a grin and tried not to breathe. Just when I thought we were going to get away with it, Agung called out, **'Me take picture!'** and toddled off around the front to take a portrait of us. How

was he capable of using the camera on his phone? When I took him shopping once, he added the prices up with a bamboo abacus for crying out loud!

'**Smile!**' said Agung.

Which of course we couldn't, as we were too busy being terrified. All the shouting attracted Ged's attention and he came lumbering over, right up close.

'**Is that you, Yip?**' he rasped, with his lardy waffle breath.

I nearly barfed!

'It *is* you, isn't it?' he said.

I kept up the pretence of being a wax dummy for another millisecond, then blinked. **DAMN!**

'Yep, it's me,' I squeaked.

He tramped around to the back of the photo board where me and Dev stood preparing for the worst. Agung and Oli watched on with intrigue.

'What are you doing here?' said Ged.

'I'm on holiday,' I replied.

I remembered the vouchers. I couldn't let Ged see them. Slyly, I pushed them deeper into my back pocket.

'What are they?'. Ged said, noticing.

'Nowt,' I mumbled.

Then Oli opened his **GINORMOUS** gaping chasm of a gob and blabbed, 'They're vouchers for **THE MEGA BEAST** ride.'

GREAT.

Ged made a lunge for them but I dodged and slid past him. There is something to be said about being small and hard to catch, especially when my life depended on it. I checked for an escape route and ran towards the aquarium. As I swerved into the car park I spotted a black box with a hinged lid. The perfect hiding place! I opened it up and shoved the envelope with the vouchers inside, thinking I could go back for them later.

MEET THE OTTERS AT SUDMOUTH AQUARIUM

NEW!

I carried on running but got stopped in my tracks. It was a dead end! It literally would be a dead end if Ged ever got his hands on me! He appeared around the corner a moment later and stalked towards me.

'Empty your pockets, Yip,' he said, blocking my exit.

I pulled out all my trouser pocket linings to show that I indeed had nothing on my person. (This was awkward as I was wearing Dev's cargo pants which I hadn't realised till now had ten thousand gazillion pockets).

As Ged took another step forward, a lady came out of the aquarium. She glanced at Ged, then at me and asked, 'You all right?'

I was too afraid to scream, 'No I am about to meet an **UNTIMELY END** in a not very attractive manner – **PLEASE HELP**!' Panicking, I spotted the sign for the Aquarium and shouted, **'OTTERS!'**

The lady looked at me weirdly (I am used to this by now), and replied **'Okaaay.'** She put on a helmet, then to my utter and indescribable horror, she got on a scooter that the perfect hiding place black box was attached to and sped off!

I couldn't tell her to stop as I didn't want to give the game away to Ged.

Thankfully he gave in and yelled, **'I'm watching you, Yip,'** then stormed off to find his granny.

Dev ran over to ask if the vouchers were safe. The *vouchers* were safe? What about *me*?! Talk about loyalty! I would have to seriously think about reevaluating our friendship when we returned to Plunkthorpe.

'A courier rode off with them,' I said, fighting the urge to collapse on the ground and eat mud in anguish.

'How the heckers did that happen?' said Dev.

I explained the story and Dev tilted his head in sympathy. 'Marshmallows?' he suggested.

Yes, marshmallows have always saved us in times of crisis, but we didn't have time to comfort eat now. We needed to get a freaking move on!

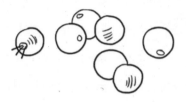

Sunday afternoon

Me and Dev rushed out of the aquarium car park to see which way the courier scooter had gone. We were just in time to see the back lights disappearing down the high street.

FANTASTIC.

Ged and his granny were nowhere to be seen. Agung was still standing by the photo board trying to get a picture of Oli on his camera, completely oblivious to the chaos. At least **THEY** were having a good time! There was a golf buggy parked by the prom and in a moment of insanity I thought about borrowing it for a kind of rubbish low-speed pursuit, even though my feet would barely reach the pedals and I had problems telling my left from my right. I didn't fancy ending up in **A&E** trussed up with a neck brace and leg splints, so I dismissed that idea pretty quickly. 'Sudmouth's only tiny, the courier can't go far,' said Dev.

'A bit like you with those harem pants on,' I replied, watching them billow like sails in the wind.

Physically I prepared myself for yet another

chase around town, but mentally all I wanted was a hot chocolate and a ten-hour foot massage in a jacuzzi. We had to get those vouchers back though. We were almost there. We couldn't risk being held up this time so I said to Oli, 'Right, you've been assigned to grandad-sitting duties again!'

'AWWW, DO I HAVE TO?' he bawled.

'Yes,' I said.

'Can I have *Magic Moo* this time?'

'Novelty balloons not involved, I'm afraid.'

'Awww, what *can* I have then?' he bawled again.

Oli was on the verge of one of his tantrums and I had to stop it before he threatened to call Mam and fabricate some story about how appallingly I was treating him. I saw a poster outside the café advertising something I knew he had wanted to try for ages.

'Ooh look,' I said. 'Why don't you get a **freakshake**?'

'I'll watch Agung if I can have one of those!' he replied, before I hardly finished my sentence.

Freakshakes are basically what a little kid would put together if you left them alone to make their own dinner. The one on the poster showed a tall glass stuffed with strawberry milkshake, chocolate ice cream, custard, whipped cream and topped with a slice of Battenberg cake. I suppose they are called **freakshakes** because they are for freaks!

Rumour has it that Poppy Plummel from school had one last year and ended up having all her top teeth replaced with a set of dentures – at the age of eleven!

Oli offered to use his birthday money to treat Agung too. I said, 'Good lad, we'll be back in half an hour and whatever you do, **DON'T MOVE**!'

Agung didn't understand what was happening so I did some shoddy sign language which probably made him think I was about to knit a balaclava and ladle soup into a wellington boot. He seemed to accept that explanation.

Translation: "Don't move."

JIGGLE

Translation: "I'll be back soon."

WIGGLE

We didn't get far before Dev's new loafers started rubbing on his heels. He had to visit the chemist for a packet of blister patches which cost three pounds ninety-nine when he could have just worn socks. Serves himself right for being such a **FASHION VICTIM**.

Halfway up the street, we saw the courier turn out of a side road and pull up at the kerb. We hid in an alley to spy on her.

'She's delivering a parcel to the greengrocer's,' I said.

'Problem is, how do we get the vouchers out of the box without looking like we're stealing them?' said Dev.

'You're the one with the expert acting skills, you tell me,' I said.

'Yeah, but I've never played the Artful Dodger, have I?'

'Well, be a **NINJA** then,' I said.

'OK, I'll do my best,' said Dev.

He adjusted his blister patch and hobbled **zombie-like** over to the vegetable display outside the shop. It was obvious he had never played a **NINJA** either! I followed swiftly behind and stood with him by the turnips, trying not to look shifty.

'Now what?' Dev whispered.

'Why don't you keep an eye on the courier, while *I* get the vouchers out of the box?' I said, thinking Dev's wounded feet would ultimately ruin the proceedings.

'OK,' said Dev. 'Right now she's chatting to the greengrocer, now she's handing him the parcel, now she's sniffing a coconut . . .'

'I don't need a running commentary!' I said.

To be honest, I was curious as to why she was sniffing a coconut, but there was no time for questions – we were **NiNJAS**!

'Tell me when she's on her way out,' I said, as I crept towards the scooter.

As I was about to stick my hand in the box, someone shouted out, **'STOP, THIEF!'** I scarpered but Dev caught his harem pants on the edge of a shelf and a billion turnips came avalanching down. Two old ladies who had previously been fondling the pongy root vegetables were now recoiling in terror, as if they had suddenly turned into hand grenades. The greengrocer came out with a face like one of his turnips - purple and **gnarled with fury**, while the courier tried not to skid on any going back to her scooter and sped off. It was turnip hell!

'PICK THAT UP OR YOU'RE PAYING FOR THE LOT!' he shouted at Dev.

I felt bad leaving Dev to tidy the mess on his own, but to be fair, if it hadn't been for his flamboyant fashion faux pas, this wouldn't have happened. Anyway, I needed to keep up with the courier.

It wasn't long before I saw the scooter again, this time outside a sandwich shop. I peered through the window. The courier was stopping to eat a bacon butty. Enough time for us to consider our next steps carefully. I texted Dev on my mobile to tell him where I was and he appeared seconds later.

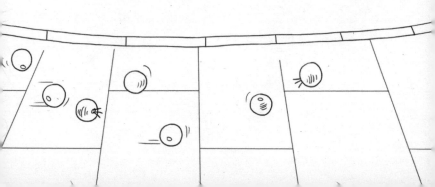

'Didn't take long for you to pick up a billion turnips,' I said.

'The greengrocer said my pants were scaring away the customers, so he let me off.'

So his pants had their uses, after all. I noticed the bag Dev insisted on carrying with him everywhere and had a **BRILLIANT IDEA.**

'Hey, Dev. Why don't you pretend to faint ever so melodramatically and have the entire contents of your bag spill across the pavement. Then, while all the passers-by rush to your aid, I can nab the vouchers.'

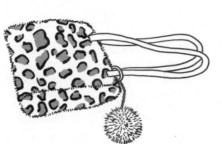

Dev screwed his face up. 'I've got all my precious things in here. I don't want complete strangers touching them.'

'Believe me, nobody will want to touch your stuff,' I said, having some idea of the junk he kept in there.

It only took another five seconds to talk him into doing the fainting thing because he is a **natural born show-off** and thinks that every other person is a talent scout that will discover him and turn him into an overnight star. He called out, **'Oh my days, I've come over all weak as a kitten!'** and flung himself to the ground so convincingly that even *I* was ready to sprint over and resuscitate him. While the unsuspecting public went to help, I sidled over to the scooter and carefully lifted up the box lid. The envelope was still safely tucked away inside.

'CALL 999!' someone shouted.

If I didn't act quickly, we were going to end up on the front page of the ***Sunday Suds*** again, but for all the wrong reasons. I grabbed the envelope, stuck it in my pocket and rushed over to help Dev.

'IT'S ALL RIGHT, EVERYONE!' I said, pushing my way through the crowd. **'HE SUFFERS FROM A DEBILITATING FOOT CONDITION.'**

Otherwise known as 'blisters'.

'But . . . the young girl has *fainted*,' said an old lady, mistaking the voluminous harem pants for a ballroom gown.

Dev could have played it up a bit longer but instead he scraped everything back into his bag (including his slip-on roller skates?!), bounced up and cried, 'It's a miracle!'

AMAZING.

What was really amazing though, was that against all odds, we'd got our vouchers back.

Sunday – late afternoon

Back at the prom we headed straight for the café to tell Agung and Oli the excellent news. We hadn't been gone that long so I figured they were probably still digging into their hideous **freakshakes**.

But when we walked in, there was no sign of them. Just a group of builders inhaling platters of all-day breakfasts and a woman feeding her whippet a custard slice.

I had instructed Oli not to move but I should have learned by now that he always does the opposite of what I tell him. It is *infuriating*.

'Maybe they've gone for a little lie-down after all that sugar,' said Dev.

'I'm the one that needs a flipping lie-down!' I said, patting my sweaty brow with a napkin.

'Why don't you call them?' said Dev.

'Good idea,' I replied, fumbling for my phone.

I dialled Agung's doddery old person's phone, but he didn't pick up.

GREAT.

What was the point of having a portable communication device if he never used it?!

I calmed myself down by thinking about gerbils sitting in eggcups. It was proving quite effective, so I added on a few tuxedos, monocles and daisy hats. **CUUUUUUTE**.

'Maddy . . .' shouted Dev. **'MADDY!'**

'Oh sorry, I was daydreaming,' I said.

'About what?'

'You *really* don't need to know,' I told him.

Dev agreed and said, 'Listen, if we want to get on **THE MEGA BEAST**, we need to find Agung and Oli, like NOW.'

'What about your gammy foot?' I asked.

'Don't worry, I've got it covered, literally,' said Dev, showing me a dozen layers of blister patches stuck over his wound.

We couldn't work out where to search first. They wouldn't have gone to the high street. They had run out of things to sniff and prod ages ago. And they couldn't be on the beach as Oli had the same dislike of sand-in-between-toes chafing as me.

Then I had a thought. 'Do you know what I reckon?' I said.

'That the earth is flat?' said Dev.

'No.'

'That the moon is made of cheese?'

'NO.'

199

'That the Tooth Fairy doesn't exist?'

'HOW VERY DARE YOU!'

Sometimes the nonsense that comes out of that lad's mouth makes me want to put a bucket over his head and bang it repeatedly with a wooden spoon until he sees sense.

'What then?' he asked.

'I reckon Agung's gone on the hunt for **pickled eggs**,' I said.

It had been ages since his last one so he was probably getting withdrawal symptoms. Plus I know he was excited to go into a chippy and ask for one since he'd learned how to say it in English. However, Sudmouth was full of chippies and I wasn't aware of their exact locations, (which was ironic as I could list every single newsagent's in town with their precise map grid markings).

The BEST WAYS to find chippies

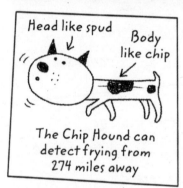

Head like spud
Body like chip

The Chip Hound can detect frying from 274 miles away

Ask any pensioner walking down the street

Next left, bear right at lights

Look for circling killer seagulls

THE PLAICE

Look it up on t'interweb

DELIVERY IN 5 SECONDS

It was a long shot but we went into the tourist information office and asked the man behind the counter if he had a map of all the fish and chip shops in Sudmouth.

'Of course!' he said. 'It's our most popular sightseeing tour.'

It is a sad situation when visitors turn up to a BEAUTY SPOT just to marvel at its saveloys and spam fritters.

The man handed over the map and remarked, 'Got a craving, have we?'

Yeah, a craving to give Oli the almightiest lecture when I laid my hands on him! We thanked the man and studied the map. There were eight chippies in total spread across town. It wouldn't take long to check them all if we were quick about it.

The first one we arrived at was a few doors along on the prom. I asked the lady if she'd seen an old codger with a dimwit young lad. She laughed and said she knew hundreds of people that matched that description and could I narrow it down. I said the young lad had a doll and possibly a beard made out of chocolate ice-cream and Battenberg cake and she replied, **'Oh no, we don't get weirdos in here,'** which was of no help whatsoever.

They weren't in the second or third chippy either. All that walking around and smell of food made me hungry so I stopped for a bag of chips in the fourth place. We sat by the window where we could keep an eye out. A moment later the land train trundled past with a bunch of passengers on board. Dev rubbed some steam off the window and waved theatrically as it went by.

'HEY,' I shouted, grabbing Dev's arm and dropping chips all down my top. **'IT'S THEM!'**

'Who?' said Dev.

'Snow White and the Seven Dwarves . . . **WHO DO YOU THINK, YOU DOUGHNUT?!'**

There they were, sitting in the second-to-last carriage, waving back like they were blumming royalty! I sprinted outside and shouted at them to get off at the next stop. Neither of them took the blindest bit of notice of me. Oli **picked his nose** while Agung chomped on his **pickled egg** (so my theory was right, he *had* gone to stuff his face with those minging things!)

Dev came running out of the chippy.

'You got your skates in there?' I asked, tugging his bag.

'Yeah,' Dev replied, puzzled.

'Get them out, **I'LL PUT THEM ON**!' I said.

'Why?'

'COS I'VE GOT TO STOP THOSE TWO PILLOCKS, THAT'S WHY!'

Dev grimaced and said, 'Shall I call ahead and warn the hospital now?'

I was tempted to say yes, but who knows, I could have been a **secret roller-skating champion** with a hidden talent just waiting to burst out!

'Don't worry, I'll be fine,' I spluttered, strapping the skates on and scrambling to my feet.

I steadied myself on a lamp post, gingerly stood upright and slowly made my way down the street. I might as well have been skidding about on a frozen oil pond with two greased-up tea trays strapped to my buttered feet. As a precaution I should have taped a duvet around my head to prevent skull fractures, but there was no time to think about such trivial matters.

The train stopped at one of the designated 'hop off' points outside **Spend A Penny Pasties**, a public toilet now converted into an artisan pasty outlet. Agung and Oli didn't get off like I'd told them to but I could make my way over now they were stationary. I was slightly peeved to discover that Dev was ahead of me because it turns out, walking with blistered feet proved to be quicker than wearing skates. I blamed the uneven cobblestones.

I had just got to the train when it started pulling away. Quickly I grabbed onto a hand rail and hitched a ride. I pulled myself along the side of the train until I found Agung and Oli.

'MEET . . . BACK . . . AT . . . THE PROM!' I shouted, sticking my head through the window.

With that I let go of the train before my kneecaps shattered, rolled to the kerbside and crashed into Keith the unofficial litter warden, who spilled rubbish all over the pavement. I didn't have time for that plum again, so I got up and skated as fast as I could away from the 'grime' scene – **HA! HA!**

When I got to the prom I was relieved to find Agung and Oli waiting. Surely this was the end of our nightmares. It better had been because it was almost the end of our holiday! I was about to give Oli that lecture I had promised myself to say but then saw the time on the prom clock. It was half four – half an hour left until the amusement park closed!

  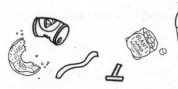

Sunday – 4.31 p.m.

All we had to do was get into the amusement park without:

a) Anyone going walkies off to distant lands

b) Getting hassled by meat-head Ged

c) Incidents relating to silly clothes, bulbous rolling vegetables or open sores

How to have a SUCCESSFUL day

Avoid incidents relating to...

GUST

Silly clothes ✓

Bulbous rolling vegetables ✓

SCAB FIX

PUSTUL-O

Open sores ✓

Meat-head Ged ✓

And we needed to do it quick. I was going to say we had to get our skates on but I already did – **HA! HA!**

When I gave Dev's skates back he pointed out a few scratches, but showed absolutely zero concern about the fact that I could have ended up in stitches (the needle and thread kind, not roaring with laughter kind).

He tutted and said, 'That's the last time you're borrowing my skates.'

'Funny that,' I answered. 'I was going to say the same thing myself. Borrow *your* skates, I mean, not you borrow mine. Because I don't have any, obviously.'

This carried on for a while until Oli shouted, **'STOP IT, I'VE GOT A HEADACHE!'**

I'm sure that was down to the preposterous amounts of sugar he'd consumed today though and nothing to do with mine and Dev's bickering.

Eventually we found ourselves standing in the ticket queue for the third time in as many days. It was beginning to feel like torture. **Actually**, getting my toenails pulled out by a crab getting *its* toenails pulled out simultaneously would have been more pleasant. To add to the agony, there was a family of fourteen at the front of the queue trying to work out the most cost-effective ticket combinations. Not with a calculator either, but by counting on their fingers. I heard them saying things like, 'No, two and two isn't five, **you dunce**!' And, '**How** can I **count** up to twelve? I've only got **ten fingers**!'

FANTASTIC.

The whole process was taking the same amount of time as Neptune does to orbit the sun (FYI, one hundred and sixty-five Earth years), so Dev decided to step in with some of his ear-splitting **soprano singing** in a bid to hurry them up and get them out of there. It turned out he didn't need to in the end as the youngest of the clan did a horribly **SMELLY POO** in his nappy and everybody abandoned the queue, leaving the mam to single-handedly sort out the mess. Now that's what I call family spirit.

This meant we were now at the front – **AT LAST!**

We bought our tickets and walked straight

through the entrance gates without a hitch. After a group high five where we all managed to miss each other's hands due to lack of coordination, we joined *another* queue for **THE MEGA BEAST**. We were close enough to see the faces of the passengers zooming past. I couldn't quite work out what their expressions were, but I was guessing it was a mixture of surprise, awe and sickening vertigo.

By gesturing, I explained to Agung that while we were on the ride, he was to wait for us at the bottom, and when it finished, we would get off and meet him. I did a wavy motion to indicate the ride but all I got back was, **'Ahhhh Macarena!'** Which I was quite offended by as I absolutely loathe that cheesy dance song and would never dream of attempting the moves.

Then, over Agung's shoulder, I saw the thing I dreaded more than double maths on a Monday morning . . . Ged Sponger. At the Hook a Duck stall.

BRILLIANT.

'Ged alert! Ged alert!' I hissed to Dev.

We both crouched behind Agung, who is the size of Yoda and far too small to use as a human shield so that was a mistake. Ged started walking in our direction, and I did the thing I was not supposed to do and made direct eye contact.

'Oi, Yip!' he shouted. 'Are you asking for trouble or what?!'

Eeeekkkkk!!!

MEGA BEAST

I thought about shouting back, 'What,' but the joke would have been lost on the daft wassock, plus winding him up would not have been a wise move. Not when we were so close to getting on the ride.

220

I was about to bolt, when his granny grabbed him by the sleeve and yanked him away, saying, 'Look over there, it's **crazy golf.** Let's have a game. You know how much I love beating you!'

Weirdly Ged seemed overpowered by his six-and-a-half-stone granny and skulked off behind her. **PHEW**, that was lucky. That golf course did look easy though, so it wouldn't be long before they finished and Ged was on the loose again!

When **THE MEGA BEAST** pulled in for the next lot of passengers, we were still nowhere near the front. Oli was hungry again (I am sure that boy has got worms). He asked for some *candy floss* from the stall opposite. *Candy floss* wasn't going to fill him up, he might as well eat dust! I didn't want to argue at this crucial point though so I said, 'OK, but Agung's coming with me. Dev and Oli, wait here.' It was better that Agung and Oli were separated this time.

I said no cheating!

PROD

On the way to the **candy floss** stall I peeked through the railings of the crazy golf course. I could see Ged's granny prodding him with her club and making him retake his shots. He didn't half look miserable!

I bought everyone a **candy floss** except for myself. If you ask me, burnt-flavoured belly button fluff that clings to your eyebrows every time you take a bite has never been particularly enticing. Dev was ecstatic to be offered one though. Mainly because the last time he had one, he didn't get to eat it because it got nicked by an alpaca at the Blogworth Agricultural Show.

On the way back to the queue, I was trying my best to stop the cloud-like *candy floss* from wafting away. When I looked up, Agung had disappeared . . . again!

BRILLIANT.

I scanned the surrounding area but couldn't see him anywhere. The only way he could have moved that quickly is if he'd teleported, which led me to believe he actually *was* Yoda.

'Agung's gone AWOL again,' I said to Dev. (That means *absent without leave*.)

'Tell me you're having a laugh,' he said.

I pointed solemnly to my not-laughing-at-all face and he soon got the message.

Dev clambered onto the railings and looked around. **'There he is!'** he yelled, pointing to the front of the queue.

'What's he doing there?' I said.

'It looks like he's . . . yes! He's getting on the ride!'

'Now *you're* having a laugh,' I said to Dev.

I gave Oli all the *candy floss* to hold and climbed on the railings next to Dev. He was right, Agung was getting on **THE MEGA BEAST**! He didn't have his specs on as usual, so he must have mistaken the front of the queue for the back. (I often did that with **FUZZFACE**, so I couldn't talk.) Somehow the ride operator was letting him on. I had to stop him! Agung would never survive a ride with three corkscrews, five bumps and a twenty-metre drop! It would be like shoving him in the washing machine on the 'Heavy Soil' setting. I tell you what, I wouldn't be surprised if he was 'heavily soiled' after getting on **THE MEGA BEAST**, that's for sure!

I jumped down and tried to work my way to the front of the queue, but there was a bloke in

front of me who was six foot five and built like an elephant. I might as well have been trying to scale **Mount Everest.** All we could do was watch helplessly as the ride started up . . . and hoped Agung didn't have a heart attack!

Sunday – 4.49 p.m.

I clasped my hands over my face in horror and watched through a millimetre gap between my fingers as Agung rode past. He was sat right at the front. **WHAT A NUTTER!** I heard a strangled squealing cry for help and felt compelled to dive on to the ride to rescue him . . . until I realised it was coming from me. I checked to see if Agung was properly strapped in, which he was – good. The last thing the whole park wanted was to witness a Yoda stunt double being flung half a mile over the treetops. I had visions of him landing in the *candy floss* machine and emerging like a Muppet version of a **swamp monster**. I imagined that news headline would be a million times more sensational than the UFO/balloon sightings.

The first corkscrew was coming up around the bend. *I* was going around the bend, more like! Agung was grinning from ear to ear, so it was fairly obvious he hadn't the faintest clue what was about to happen. There is something to be said about being extremely short-sighted. He copied the young lad next to him by holding his arms up in the air. Me, Oli and Dev winced. We hoped we could get him back home in one piece.

Just then my mobile phone rang. I thought it might be the amusement park security asking if I was the one responsible for letting a vulnerable pensioner onto the ride without a ticket. I was formulating an excuse about how I had never met this **geriatric daredevil** in my life, when I saw it was Dad's name on the screen. My parents don't half choose the worst times to call – or maybe there never *was* a good time to call because my life was so permanently **BARKING MAD!** I hadn't spoken to my parents all day so I thought I'd better pick up.

'Do acting, do normal!' mouthed Dev, when he saw me answer it.

'Hi, Dad!' I said, in a voice that sounded like

I'd just inhaled too much helium.

'Hey, Maddy, are you all having a good time?' he said.

At that precise moment, Agung was upside down and laughing his chops off. I was dreading his teeth falling out. What if they fell into the moving parts below and broke the machinery? Emergency services wouldn't have enough ladders to cope with rescuing so many passengers dangling that high up in mid-air.

'Yeah, we're having a *wild* time!' I replied, trying to sound excited.

'When are we expecting you lot home then?' he asked.

Not for a while if we have a denture fail, I thought.

'Tonight at seven,' I said.

Just then Mam yelled out in the background, **'Ask if they want tofu stew or flaxseed pie for their tea!'**

Right then was **NOT** the time to discuss meal options! Especially ones that were so vomit-inducing.

'Your Mam says . . .'

'Yes, I heard, thanks, Dad,' I said.

I chose tofu stew and immediately felt more sick in the stomach than I already was.

Agung was hurtling towards us again. He was now holding something in his hand. When he got closer, I noticed that it was in fact, a **pickled egg**! How could he do casual snacking while being accelerated with a G-force equivalent to a **space shuttle** launching?

I noticed a crowd had gathered and were cheering him on. One young girl was even holding up a cardboard placard with GO, GRANDAD! written in felt-tip pen on it. He had a full-on fan club going on!

'AGUNG'S FLYING - WHEEEEEE!' shouted Oli, as he went past.

I put my hand over Oli's mouth to stop him blabbing any more.

Dad heard him and asked, 'What was that?'

'Um . . . It's Oli. He's bursting for a *wee*. I better sort him out,' I babbled.

'Well, you better get on with it then. See you at seven,' said Dad.

I was relieved to hang up but there was still the crisis of Agung to deal with. And if that wasn't bad enough, I spotted Ged coming out of the crazy golf course too! He made a beeline for us.

GREAT.

From the other side of the railings he eyed up the *candy floss* Oli was still holding and said, 'Gis us your *candy floss*.'

'Mmmmmph, mmmph,' mumbled Oli.

I wondered why Oli was being so quiet: turned out I still had my hand over his big fat gob.

'Hey, Ged,' said Dev, trying to stall him. **'I bet you'll like this floss more!'** Then he clenched his fists and started swinging his arms furiously from side to side to the front and back of his body. Dev is the best at flossing. I am dead jealous.

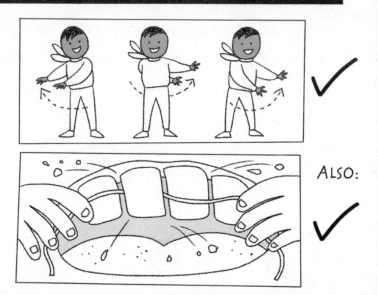

How to be completely BRILL at flossing

Ged stood hypnotised for a moment. Then he shook his head dizzily and snarled, 'Gis us your *candy floss* or I'll come over the railing and **get it myself**.'

I prayed for a miracle to save us. A second later I heard a familiar voice. It was Derek chatting to someone next to the Ball and Bucket Toss. He had *Princess* with him. I remembered Derek telling us about *Princess*'s obsession with anything sweet and the most excellent idea sprang to mind. I was unable to verbally communicate my most excellent idea to Dev but luckily, due to being bezzies for so long our minds had synced like conjoined twins, so we automatically knew what the other was thinking most of the time. (Not always a great gift I might add, as Dev thinks mostly about satin capes and blousons).

'Yeah, OK then, let's give him the **candy floss**,' said Dev.

I took the **candy floss** off Oli, making sure to waft them about a bit.

Oli's mouth gaped open in disbelief and his chin started wobbling dangerously. I think if I had let Oli carry on with a full-on screaming tantrum, that would have been enough to scare off Ged on its own. But I wanted to carry out *my* plan.

I said to Ged, 'You might as well have them cos we're getting on the ride in a mo and we're not allowed to eat on there.' (Even though Agung was zooming over our heads in full view with a **pǐckled egg** in hand.)

I could see **Princess** sniffing the air as I handed them over to Ged. She had caught wind of the **candy floss**, just as we expected! Her floppy head shot up when she spotted the huge mound of pink fluffy treats Ged was now

Hey, is she talking about Ged?

brandishing. She galloped over, picking up the speed of a **hurtling juggernaut**. Fortunately Ged hadn't the foggiest what was coming up behind him, so the next thing he knew, he was knocked down and forcefully pinned to the ground. *Princess* proceeded to snaffle the *candy floss*, drowning Ged in a lake of saliva while she did so.

The crowd that had been watching Agung with morbid interest was now gawking at Ged's granny going berserk trying to bat **Princess** off with her handbag. Me and Dev laughed so hard, snot came flying out and Oli nearly did end up weeing himself!

In the meantime, **THE MEGA BEAST** pulled back onto the platform. Agung got off looking a bit windswept but with a massive smile on his face. It was good to see his teeth were still in. As he stepped onto the platform a few people patted him on the back like he'd just won the **Monaco Grand Prix**.

Frantically, I waved and gestured for him to stay where he was. He couldn't see me though, so I pretended I was swatting a *mosquito*.

242

It was a good job the amusement park had a ten-foot perimeter fence around it. That way Agung could be contained!

The queue shuffled forward. It was our turn now! We were just in time for the last ride – talk about close. But as we approached, horror of horrors, the barrier came down in front of us and we were refused entry! The last ride of the day was full.

NOOOOOOO!!!!!

Sunday – park closing time

All my dreams crumbled like dust before me. Behind us in the queue, at least another ride full of passengers were shaking their fists at the sheer injustice, while I just wanted to crawl quietly under a bush and die.

'This can't be true,' I muttered.

'No it is not and I'll make sure of it!' snapped Dev, and before I knew it he'd ducked under the barrier and started quibbling with the ride operator.

Pwetty please?

'Please,' he pleaded, thinking up some dramatic excuse. 'I've worked fifteen Saturday jobs to save up for this ride.'

'Yeah, well here's **another job** for ya . . . get **back** behind the **barrier**!' said the operator.

Glumly, Dev ducked back under. At least he tried.

Agung was by the exit on the far side. He was surrounded by admirers shaking his hand and arranging elaborate group selfies. **'AGUNG!'** I shouted. He heard me this time and headed towards us.

He chuckled, **'Hao gow!'**

That means 'so much fun' in Hakka. The last time he said that, **FUZZFACE** had smashed two vases and pulled down a curtain trying to catch a fly. Dad had told me what it meant.

'Do you know that man?' the operator said to me.

I wasn't sure whether admitting it was going to get me into trouble, but hell, things couldn't have got any worse than they were already.

'Erm, yeah, he's my grandad,' I said.

'This man is a flippin' hero!' said the operator, patting Agung on the shoulder. 'He's

248

the oldest bloke we've ever had on any ride here, let alone **THE MEGA BEAST**. He didn't have a ticket but he had a voucher, so that was good enough for me.'

Then I saw: Agung was holding a page of the **Sudmouth Post** that his pickled eggs were wrapped in. The voucher was clearly printed on one side.

'**Pickle egg,**' said Agung, waving it in my face.

'You know what?' said the operator. 'I was so impressed with your old gramps here that I'm going to let you lot have a go on the ride too.'

'Hello? Hello?' I repeated to myself. 'Earth

calling Maddy.' I needed to test my hearing because I couldn't quite believe what the operator had just said.

'Cor, thanks, Mister!' said Oli, giving the man a high five with Luke's microscopic hand.

'Thank you, kind sir!' cried Dev.

In my excitement I embarrassingly blurted out, **LOVE YOU!** But thankfully everyone pretended not to hear.

The ride slowed down and pulled into the platform to let the last lot of passengers off. I was so excited. We were inches away from climbing aboard the most awesome ride in the history of awesome rides! It seemed like a century ago when we first saw the poster advertising it in the **PLUNKTHORPE NINETY-NINE PENCE SHOP**. The operator let just me, Oli and Dev through the barrier – much to the disgust of everyone behind us in the queue. It was to be a VIP exclusive!

Agung sat next to me at the front while Oli and Dev settled behind, then down came the safety harnesses – this was it! The roller coaster cruised along to the first bend and made its slow ascent. From there I looked down and saw Ged getting wiped down with a hanky, spat on by his granny. He had a face like a smacked bum – **HA!**

We sped up as we approached the first corkscrew then, without warning, it spun around so hard, my innards nearly spewed out from my mouth. There was no time to ponder over whether I liked the experience, as the next **corkscrew** came immediately after.

'UUNNGGH!'

'OOOF!'

'WHOAAA!'

'EEEEEEK!'

'SOMEONE SAVE ME!'

A few seconds after *that* we were catapulted around yet another **corkscrew**. I counted three **corkscrews** so at least that bit was over with! I just had enough time to push my eyeballs back into their sockets when we hurtled over five steep bumps.

'How on earth is **THIS** hao gow?!' I shouted at Agung, who was shrieking with joy.

When my spinal column eventually realigned itself, we were tilted upright sharply and began to climb. Why wasn't the **TORTURE** over with yet?! Why did I ever agree to this?! This was Dev's idea. I made a note to have stern words with him afterwards if:

a) I was still alive

b) He was still alive

I looked over at Agung and he was having the time of his life! Maybe I would have been too if I was as bonkers as him. We stopped at the top of the sheer twenty-foot drop finale.

Then . . .

We screamed like lemmings plunging off a cliff as we tore downwards.

'It's been nice . . . **KNOWING YOUUUUUU**!' I yelled to everyone I ever knew and loved.

Then we braked and were upright again. I opened my eyes and pinched myself. I was still alive – how could that be? The ride slowed, pulled over to the platform edge and finally came to a halt.

My legs were like jelly as I clambered out. Oli was the same shade of green as our **B&B** bathroom suite and Dev couldn't even speak – well, there's always a first time for everything, so they say!

'Enjoy that?' said the operator, as we staggered down the steps.

'Need . . . lie . . . down,' was all I could croak back.

'Me . . . too,' said Oli, gagging slightly.

Dev answered with a limp thumbs up.

Agung, jolly as ever, shook the operator's hand and gave him his last pɪckled egg as a gesture of goodwill.

We were so shook up that the trek back to the **B&B** felt like we were being tossed about on a dinghy in a force ten gale. After packing

(as in shoving everything into our bags aimlessly), it took all our collective effort to thank Derek and Wendy and give **𝓟𝓻𝓲𝓷𝓬𝓮𝓼𝓼** a pat without being sick in their parlour palm plant pot.

During the journey home on the bus, we stared blankly out of the window the whole way, not saying a word to each other, while Agung happily chatted away in Chinese.

When we arrived in Plunkthorpe square, Dad was already there waiting to pick us up.

'Good time?' he said, as we tumbled into the car.

We answered with various grunts.

'What's the matter with you lot? You look like you've seen a **GHOST**,' Dad chuckled.

Agung entered into a long explanation to Dad in Chinese, then they both laughed heartily for much longer than was necessary.

As soon as Dad pulled into our driveway, Dev jumped out of the car, declared tragically, **'I may be gone for some time,'** turned on his heel, and dashed into his house.

The rest of us went inside our house where I was greeted with the 'comforting' aroma of tofu stew, which made me feel even more nauseous. Mam came out of the kitchen and hugged me so hard I thought I was actually going to hurl down the front of her apron.

'Take your shoes off before you go upstairs,' she said. 'I don't want the **new carpet** ruined, especially as it's all ready for the **childminding inspectors** coming this week!'

Forget the carpet, I thought. *I'm the one that's ruined!*

To add to the cheek, Jack asked, 'Did you bring any **pressies** back?'

I replied, 'Yes, as a matter of fact, I did.'

I presented Dad with his fudge, Mam with her lentils, then took the **Sunday Suds** out of my bag. 'A special souvenir for you,' I said. I knew it would make him well jealous.

'**Aww, you jammy git!** Did you see them?' Jack gasped, scanning the front-page UFO article.

I grinned slyly. 'So close, you wouldn't believe.'

HA! That shut him up.

At dinner, Dad told Mam and Jack about our unfortunate experience. Jack was in one of his annoying smug moods, as Kayla had invited him round to meet her parents while he was staying at Gav's next door to hers. I hope they took one look at Jack's **croissant-shaped zits** and talked her into having more approvable friends.

Jack was in **HYSTERICS** when he found out how ill we felt after the ride, whereas Mam was more sympathetic and only snorted once. That is until Agung showed her the picture he'd taken of us in the seafront photo board, just before Ged almost killed me, then she almost **CHOKED** on her tofu, **CRACKING** up. I'm glad everyone else found it funny.

After Mam finally composed herself, she said to me and Oli, 'Good news, we're planning on doing the downstairs carpets as well now . . .'

She hesitated.

'And?' we replied.

'Well, we reckon it would be a brilliant idea if you went back to Sudmouth. What do you think about that?'

The end